MAIDEN & MODEST

MAIDEN & MODEST

A Renaissance Pastoral Romance

BERNARDIM RIBEIRO

Translated from the Portuguese by

GREGORY RABASSA

Foreword by Earl E. Fitz

TAGUS PRESS AT UMASS DARTMOUTH

Dartmouth, Massachusetts

ADAMASTOR SERIES 8
Tagus Press at UMass Dartmouth
www.portstudies.umassd.edu
© 2012 Gregory Rabassa
Manufactured in the United States of America
General Editor: Frank F. Sousa
Managing Editor: Mario Pereira
Designed by Richard Hendel
Typeset in Garamond Premier Pro and Celestia
by Tseng Information Systems, Inc.

Tagus Press books are produced and distributed for
Tagus Press by University Press of New England, which is a
member of the Green Press Initiative.
The paper used in this book meets their minimum requirement
for recycled paper.

Publication of this book was made possible in part
by a grant from the Luso-American Foundation.

For all inquiries, please contact:
Tagus Press at UMass Dartmouth
Center for Portuguese Studies and Culture
285 Old Westport Road
North Dartmouth MA 02747-2300
Tel. 508-999-8255
Fax 508-999-9272
www.portstudies.umassd.edu

Library of Congress Cataloging-in-Publication Data
Ribeiro, Bernardim, 1482–1552.
Maiden and modest: a renaissance pastoral romance / Bernardim Ribeiro;
translated from the Portuguese by Gregory Rabassa; foreword by Earl E. Fitz.
p. cm. — (Adamastor series; 8)
ISBN 978-1-933227-37-5 (cloth: alk. paper)
I. Rabassa, Gregory. II. Title.
PQ 9231.R46 2012
869.3′3 — dc23   2012001093

5 4 3 2 1

CONTENTS

✳ ✳ ✳
✳ ✳
✳

FOREWORD

Among the many gems of Portuguese literature, Bernardim Ribeiro's *Menina e Moça* (1554; *Maiden and Modest* 2012) stands out as one of the most resplendent. Though long admired by those of us fortunate enough to toil away within the rich and diverse Luso-Brazilian tradition, *Maiden and Modest* is now beginning to catch the attention of scholars who labor in the vineyards of the European Renaissance generally. Well acquainted with the poetry of the great Camões and the theater of Gil Vicente, these modern students of the Renaissance can now turn their attention to another extraordinary Portuguese literary achievement, this time in the realm of narrative art. Happily, Portuguese letters are slowly but surely gaining the international recognition and respect that they deserve, and the appearance of *Maiden and Modest*, in a superb English translation by Gregory Rabassa, will most assuredly hasten this process along.

Written by a man but in a woman's voice, Ribeiro's mid-sixteenth-century masterpiece adds considerably to our understanding of European and Iberian narrative fiction in the era immediately preceding the appearance of *Don Quixote* (Pt. I, 1605; Pt. II, 1615) and what is widely regarded as the birth of the modern novel. For Aubrey F. G. Bell, in fact, *Maiden and Modest* stands as "the earliest and best of those pastoral romances which led Don Quixote to contemplate a quieter sequel to his first adventures" (Bell 19–20). To better appreciate *Maiden and Modest* and what it contributes to the development of the novel form, we do well to consider both the importance of Ribeiro's text within its own national tradition and its relevance to the larger Renaissance tradition to which it belongs. Seen from this comparative context, numerous important features of *Maiden and Modest* stand out: its cultivation of a self-conscious text and narrator/protagonists; its implementation of a style that waxes both realistic and poetic; its keen appreciation of nature; its entwining of Christian Humanism and Iberian politics with issues of Jewish mysticism, cultural identity, and history; its blending of differing levels, registers, and modes of discourse; its handling of time; its creation of inter-connecting tales that reflect and enrich each other; its multiple parallelisms; its word play; its surprising consciousness of what we today term gender; its carefully delineated and, in part, psychologically driven characters; its adroit use of dialogue; its effective use of irony, symbolism, and ambiguity; and, finally, its development of the reader's role in deciphering the different codes and cues employed and in establishing the various meanings of the events narrated.

In considering these and other features of his work, it is clear that Ribeiro is steeped in both the Portuguese and European traditions he makes use of and that he is an important innovator in terms of the new themes and techniques he elects to explore. The impact of Italian letters seems especially strong in his work, and commentators have long felt that echoes not only of Dante and the *Dolce Stil Nuovo* but also of the love poetry of Petrarch animate *Maiden and Modest*. Even Boccaccio, by way of his *Fiammetta*, has been linked to Ribeiro, with the result that a modern critic might well regard the Portuguese text as a Renaissance sentimental novel that is basically gynocentric in orientation, bucolic in nature, and, if not quite tragic, then certainly disenchanted in its treatment of love as a unifying force in human affairs (Salgado Júnior; Amado 28–29; Malaca Castelheiro; Carrasco González 2008: 38).

As Helder Macedo has shown, it seems likely that Bernardim Ribeiro (1482?–1552) was a Portuguese Jew who, early in the sixteenth century, converted to Christianity for the material benefit that would have likely accrued to him for having done so but who, later in life, re-embraced his Jewish heritage (Macedo 24). This bit of biographical speculation, while not entirely verifiable (Carrasco González 2008: 20–21), has a parallel in the narrative by way of the apostate *cavaleiro* who changes his name to Binmarder (an anagram for Bernardim) and who, in the process (which also involves disguising himself as a simple rustic), effectively exchanges one identity for another. The effect of this, however, is that Binmarder immediately becomes a divided, conflicted self, just as the stream the Maiden gazes so sadly upon is divided, again in parallel fashion, by a large rock that impedes its progress. Later, and in a telling complication, our honorable *cavaleiro* shows that he is torn between his loveless though monetarily beneficial allegiance to the lady Aquelísia and his dramatic change of allegiance to the beautiful Aónia, whose love will be his only reward. Although much of Ribeiro's life remains a mystery, modern scholarship suggests that *Maiden and Modest* carries a strong autobiographical streak within it, one that, if the reader is willing to extrapolate a bit from the text, offers some very interesting reflections on the larger social, political, and religious conflicts of the author's turbulent time and place.

Seeing traces of both the Cabala and the Zohar in *Maiden and Modest*, Macedo, for example, avers that Ribeiro's narrative develops the theme of exile, so fundamental to Jews after their traumatic expulsion from Spain in 1492, in the context of Binmarder's drama. The theme of exile was likewise fundamental, Macedo claims, to Ribeiro's own, personal situation (Macedo 28–30). This mixing of Judaism and Christianity in Portugal (to which as many as 120,000 Spanish Jews fled after being expelled from Ferdinand and Isabella's Spain, then newly victorious over the Moors) lends *Maiden and Modest* a hybrid quality that leavens the narrative considerably and that imbues it with deep historical and cultural significance. Under the Portuguese monarch, Dom Manuel, inter-faith marriages between *cristãos-novos* (Jews who had converted to Christianity) and *cristãos-velhos* (people of old Christian families) were officially encouraged and so it is entirely possible, even likely, that Ribeiro, given his high standing at court, would have been a participant in this particular social, political, and economic policy. At the same time, however, it was ill-advised and even dangerous to drop one's professed Christianity and re-convert to Judaism, as Ribeiro may well have done. To have done so would have required great personal courage and would have arisen from a sense of profound conviction; indeed both of these qualities infuse Ribeiro's novel, though in different ways. Socially and politically, as well as psychologically, this theme of exile, of being forced to live an alien existence and to live as a stranger in one's own land, adds depth and human pathos to what in different, less talented hands might have merely been yet another pastoral romance of chivalry and courtly manners.

Integrally connected with the text's Jewish roots is its surprising concern with what modern readers would think of as issues of gender. More than being a text written by a man in a woman's voice (a kind of writing that, via the *Cantigas de Amigo*, has a long and venerable tradition in Portuguese literature; see n. 1), *Maiden and Modest* offers a startlingly frank and psychologically acute assessment of what it meant to be a woman in the male world of knight errantry, a world heavily freighted with rigid codes of conduct, for both men and women, the latter topic constituting one of the basic *topoi* of sixteenth-century sentimental writing (Carrasco González 2008: 34). However, despite the degree to which the text emphasizes and thus legitimizes the female perspective, a careful reading of *Maiden and Modest* also reveals a thoughtful, though more muted, consideration of gender from the male point of view, of what it meant to be a man and a *cavaleiro andante* in the same culture and time period. The result is that Ribeiro's novel produces an ethos that many readers will recognize as being essentially feminist in nature, but, as with modern feminism, with relevance for women and men alike. If, for some, this reading remains open for discussion (Carrasco González 2008: 34), the seriousness with which *Maiden and Modest* treats the female condition most certainly is not, and, on balance, one feels that it emerges as the novel's single most striking feature. Macedo argues convincingly that this is indeed the case and that, for him, the novel's fundamentally feminist impulse, its distinctive voice, stems from what he sees as the unique qualities of Spanish and Portuguese Judaism of the time, qualities that, in terms of their importance to the status of women in society, he believes sets the Iberian Jewish experience apart from all other branches of Judaism (Macedo 27–28).

One of the most intriguing textual representations of this integration of the Jewish and the feminist experiences (and one seen in the contrast between the seemingly eternal mountains and the ever-protean seascape) is Ribeiro's development of the play between constancy and change, with women portrayed as being steadfast while the men are seen to be mercurial, even capricious, in thought and deed (Macedo 43, 46–48). Change, in fact, functions as one of *Maiden and Modest*'s most basic motifs and appears, in one form or another, throughout the novel. Developed, indeed, as an extended metaphor, this contrast between change and constancy leads Ribeiro's text to suggest that the stability of women (through whom Jewish traditions are passed from one generation to the next) is actually superior, morally and in terms of social stability, to the mutability (some would say the fickleness) of men (Macedo 47). In Ribeiro's deftly allusive presentation of it, however, this is a conclusion that also engages the larger, more philosophical problem of how one deals with the challenges and vicissitudes of life; in short, how one maintains a sense of integrity in a constantly changing world, a theme at the heart of the Renaissance *Weltanschauung*. The Portuguese text's remarkable gender considerations lead the reader to consider not only the particular social and political situations of the women and men dealt with here in a specific historical context, but also deeper issues of human desire, identity, and conduct that are involved. Though brief and discreet in their appearance, even issues of sexuality seem to have a place in Ribeiro's novel.

Indeed, if we wish to regard love as the glue that, thematically speaking, holds *Maiden and Modest* together and that connects its different parts, then it might be said to exist in three forms, or contexts: as a function of the sentimental novel (a genre for which, according to Alan Deyermond, Ribeiro's text may well have had something of a transforming effect); as a rather revolutionary interrogation of the situation of women, socially, politically (that is, in terms of their legal status, or agency, and the choices that were available, or not available, to them), psychologically, and sexually, in sixteenth-century Portugal (and, by extension, all of Europe); and, more diffusely, as a consideration not of a frivolous emotion or pursuit but of the complex and often frustrating ontological problem that, in truth, love is.

Although this latter category receives little or no explicit attention in the text itself, its contemplation seems a natural response by a reader attuned (as readers in Ribeiro's time would have been) to the implications of love as a paradoxical force that possesses both psychological and carnal aspects and that produces not only pleasure and life but suffering and death as well. The plight of Lady Belisa, who, married and pregnant, dies painfully in childbirth (a sobering consequence of having accepted her husband's "loving embraces"), might well be considered from this perspective, as might the text's suggestion that, in her bed at night and aroused by her passion for the close by but physically unattainable Binmarder, Aónia may resort to masturbation to satisfy her own natural urges. Read from this perspective, the story of Aónia, who is similarly enflamed with desire, would constitute a female-based parallel with Binmarder's own experience with amorous ardor. Although the text is oblique with respect to what may or may not happen in her bed, the reference to Aónia's possible act of self-satisfaction does not contain any note of censure, a point that argues strongly in favor of *Maiden and Modest*'s essential feminism. At any rate, for Ribeiro it is the theme of love, in all its myriad forms and complications, that most fully embodies the tangled issues of gender, desire, marriage, and identity, both personal and public, that the narrative explores.

Stylistically, too, *Maiden and Modest* is a remarkable document. Consisting throughout of a lyrically inclined and consistently rhythmic prose, it also manifests a variety of other very effective rhetorical features, including analepsis, pleonasms, repetition, syntactical inventiveness, antithesis, nominalized verbs, and anacoluthons (the latter imparting the subtle but pervasive sense of anxiety that characterizes the text; Saraiva and Lopes 240–41). Though Ribeiro is a respected but rather conventional poet, he is a writer who achieves real innovative brilliance only by mixing modes, in this case those of poetry and narrative. The result, in *Maiden and Modest*, is a distinctly composite text, one made up of different genres and one that freely avails itself of the techniques of poetry to develop and deepen its narrative line and move it forward. Some of *Maiden and Modest*'s more obvious poetic devices and qualities include alliteration, a heavy use of the imperfect tense (imparting an open-ended quality to the text) and the artificial passive voice, an emphasis on abstract issues (such as hope, will, fortune, and fate), and a knack for polyvalent and periphrastic constructions that, taken in aggregate, help convey the motif of change so central to the novel's plot structure and ethos (Saraiva and Lopes 241). Another, quite singular quality of Ribeiro's poetic style is the way its syntax so often parallels, expands, or intensifies the psychological states of the characters being portrayed. This is particularly prevalent in the novel's first two sections, where the clear and thoroughly engaging soliloquies of the women (the younger and the older) constitute a powerful presentation of female psychology. Although the candor of what the two women have to say, about the nature of love and about their lot as women, is what catches the eye of the reader first, a second, more stylistically sensitive reading reveals the degree to which Ribeiro's sentence structure both imparts a unique force to the women's voices and leads the reader to feel their potency. To be sure, this technique is displayed in the novel's other stories as well, though it is most prominent, and effective, in the two female discourses that open the novel.

Formally, thematically, and technically, *Maiden and Modest* is a heterogeneous work, the high point, one could argue, of the development of the sixteenth-century pastoral novel. The influence of Ribeiro's novel on other, better-known texts has become a topic of serious, systematic study in Spain (where its importance to Jorge de Montemayor is now clearly established; Carrasco González 1999), and the novel most certainly deserves a more detailed consideration as part of its larger European tradition. Unjustly overlooked in terms of its contributions to European and world literature, Portuguese literature is now demanding its place at the international literary banquet table, and the appearance, in English, of Bernardim Ribeiro's marvelous Renaissance novel makes its long overdue seating all the easier.

A few words should be said about the translation itself. Under the best of conditions, the art of translation is always a difficult task. To re-create a literary text in another language system is not merely a creative exercise in linguistic transformation (as if this were not difficult enough), it also involves issues of history, culture, interpretation, and aesthetics. And when, as here, the project involves two language systems as different as sixteenth-century Portuguese and twenty-first century English are, and when the two readerships come to their texts with such radically different expectations, the translator's task is doubly daunting. Some of the vagaries and quirks of Ribeiro's original *quinhentista* Portuguese, for example, simply have no counterpart in English and so cannot be replicated. Prominent among these are the tonal expressiveness of the Portuguese subjunctives (past, present, and future), the syntactic flexibility of the Portuguese line, and the semantic ambiguity Ribeiro wrings out of its tense sequencing, its wide-ranging verbal aspect, and the fact that, to make sense, Portuguese verbs need not show their exact subjects (as English, by way of contrast, requires). All but unanimously regarded as one of the greatest literary translators ever to pick up pen, Gregory Rabassa has given us, in his *Maiden and Modest*, a version of Ribeiro's *Menina e Moça* that is faithful to its original both in terms of content and with respect to style, the latter, so dependent on issues of diction, syntax, and euphony, being always the most elusive quality of a text to recreate. A major measure of Ribeiro's effectiveness as a writer in Portuguese comes from his ability to change registers and tones and to match his language use to the different characters, to their evolving states of mind, and to the varying circumstances in which they find themselves, and Rabassa's close but fluid rewriting of *Maiden and Modest* captures these often quicksilver and subtle shifts to an exceptional degree. That Professor Rabassa succeeds so brilliantly here in reproducing, in a supple English version, Ribeiro's very mannered Portuguese stands as yet another testament to his extraordinary talents as a reader/interpreter, translator, and writer.

My job as editor was to read the translation against the original, to make sure nothing was inadvertently left out, and to see that the English version was not only amenable to contemporary English language eyes but that it reflected, as often as possible, the semantic divagations, the rhythms, and the stylistic twists and turns of the original 1554 Portuguese text. A few notes were added in order to clarify some passages whose importance might be unclear to readers not acquainted with the Portuguese language or with Portuguese literature, culture, and history. Any slips or errors, real or perceived, are therefore to be attributed to failure on the editor's part and not as evidence of any flaws in the translation itself.

EARL E. FITZ
Vanderbilt University

WORKS CITED

Amado, Teresa. *Menina e Moça de Bernardim Ribeiro*. Lisbon: Editorial Comunicação, 1984.

Bell, Aubrey F. G. *Portuguese Literature*. Oxford: Clarendon Press, 1922.

Carrasco González, Juan M. "El origen portugués de la novela pastoril castellana." *Literatura portuguesa y literatura española: influencias y relaciones*. Ed. María Rosa Álvares Seller. València: Universitat de València, 1999. 327–345.

———. *Menina e Moça ou Saudades*. Coimbra: Angelus Novus 2008.

Deyermond, Alan. "The Female Narrator in Sentimental Fiction: *Menina e Moça* and *Clareo y Florisea*." *Portuguese Studies* 1 (1985): 47–57.

Macedo, Helder. *Menina e Moça, ou Saudades*. Lisbon: Publicações Dom Quixote, 1990.

Malaca Castelheiro, João. "A Influência da *Fiammetta* de Boccaccio na *Menina e Moça* de Bernardim Ribeiro." *Ocidente* 74 (1968): 145–68.

Martins, José Vitorino de Pina. *História de Menina e Moça: reprodução facsimilada da edição de Ferara, 1554*. Lisbon: Serviço de Educação e Bolsas & Fundação Calouste Gulbenkian, 2002.

Salgado Júnior, António. *A Menina e Moça e o Romance Sentimental no Renascimento*. Lisbon: Aveiro, 1940.

Saraiva, António José, and Óscar Lopes. *História da Literatura Portuguesa*, 6th ed. Porto: Porto Editora Limitada, 1972.

NOTE ON THE TRANSLATION

The history of the text of *Maiden and Modest* by Bernardim Ribeiro is complex and contested. Although the text has been the object of intense and comprehensive scholarly interest, it nevertheless lacks a definitive critical edition.

Five versions of the text have come down to us from the sixteenth century. The earliest extant version is a manuscript in the Biblioteca Nacional, Lisbon that dates from around 1543. The first edition of *Maiden and Modest* was printed in Ferrara, Italy, by the publisher Abraham Usque, a Portuguese Jew, in 1554. The text printed in Ferrara forms the core of all modern editions, including the present translation. A second, vastly expanded edition was printed in Évora by André de Burgos in 1557. The additional material in the Évora edition has generated much controversy because its authenticity is doubtful. A third edition, printed in Cologne, Germany, in 1559, fairly faithfully reproduces the text of the Ferrara edition. Finally, a late sixteenth-century manuscript, perhaps dating from before 1581, survives in the Real Academia de la Historia, Madrid.

The two major issues surrounding Ribeiro's text of *Maiden and Modest* concern interpretation of the seemingly unfinished nature of the text and the disputed authorship of the chapters from the Évora edition. All versions of the text, except for the Évora edition, end at the same point: the Lisbon manuscript and Ferrara edition have identical endings, while the Madrid manuscript concludes just a few lines earlier. The text of the Ferrara edition, which is common to all extant versions of the text, is certainly authentic. However, the narrative seems to end abruptly in an open-ended manner, suggesting to some scholars that the apparently interrupted text is incomplete, lacking a conclusion. Moreover, an enigmatic note in the Lisbon manuscript, claiming that the rest of Ribeiro's text is rumored to be housed in the royal palace, amplifies the controversy. Although some scholars, such as Juan Carrasco González, contend that the first seven chapters of the Évora edition might reflect a rough, unfinished draft by Ribeiro, most scholars, such as Helder Macedo and José Vitorino de Pina Martins, do not accept the chapters from the Évora edition as the authentic continuation of *Maiden and Modest*. Consequently, the present translation is based on the text of the 1554 Ferrara edition (as amended by modern editors). This is the only text that is securely and unanimously accepted as authentic by scholars.

Ribeiro's text has also been known by two different titles since the sixteenth century. The Lisbon manuscript refers to the text as the "Saudades de Bernardim Ribeira que foy autor della," whereas the Ferrara edition gives the title as "Hystoria de Menino e Moça." The translation again follows the Ferrara edition in this regard.

In order to facilitate and enhance the reading of *Maiden and Modest* by contemporary readers, the translation follows the example of other modern editions in dividing the text into four distinct stories and in separating paragraphs and altering sentences and punctuation, rendering the complex syntax of the original more accessible.

MARIO PEREIRA
University of Massachusetts Dartmouth

MAIDEN & MODEST

INTRODUCTION

1. *The Maiden's Monologue*

Maiden and modest, I was carried away from my mother's house to far-away lands. The reason for my being taken away I never knew, I was so young. There is none I can give now except that it was what was meant to be, then and later on. I had lived there just enough time so that it was impossible for me to live anywhere else. I was very happy in that land but, alas, it all changed so quickly that I have long sought it in my memory and seek it still. Fortune it was that made me sad, but fortune, too, perhaps had made me happy. After seeing so many things changed into something else, and pleasure turned into deep grief, I was saddened all the more by the good that once had held me than by the evil I now bore.

For my contentment (if such a thing there can be in the midst of such sadness and longing), I have chosen to come and spend time in these woods where the place and the lack of human conversation might calm my thoughts, for it would have been a great mistake after all the troubles I have seen with my own eyes to still hold hope for relief from the world, which has never given it to anyone. Being alone here, so far from other people and even farther from myself, from where I see nothing but the changeless mountains on one side and the ever-changing waters of the sea on the other, I thought I might forget my misfortunes and, with the help of this place and with great effort, I try as hard as I can not to leave anything in me that might bring on any greater sorrow. My whole being has been the dwelling place of grief for so long, and still is, and with good reason, for it seems that one misfortune is replaced by another, while one good has never been replaced by another good. And that is how, so strangely, I was carried off to where all my anxieties took on odd shapes before my eyes, nor were my ears left without their share of my grief.

I saw then that the pity I felt for others should have been as great as that which I felt for myself, and so taken with my sorrow was I that I seemed to be the cause of it. So strongly do I feel the basis for my own sadness, that it would seem that I never see woe but that I seek it out. It seems to me therefore that this changed circumstance in which I find myself now in this land is something I wanted as the best way to end the few days of life left me. But in this, as in so many other things, I have been misled, because it is two years already that I have been here and still I cannot determine when my final hour awaits me. It cannot be long in coming.

This makes me have doubts about writing down the things I have seen and heard. But then I thought that fear of not finishing was no reason not to start, because I would be writing only for myself alone, for whom unfinished things are no novelty, for when have I seen pleasure fulfilled or evil have an end? It appears to me, rather, that for the time that I am to be here in this wild place, as my ill fate has ordained, I could not undertake anything more to my wishes or as God wills them to be.

If this little book should find itself in the hands of happy people, let them not read it, because it might seem to them that their own situation will be as changeable as the ones told here and their pleasure will be less. Wherever I might be, this would pain me because it is quite enough that I should bear my sorrows and not share them with others for to bear. Those who are sad may read it, but it is not for men as there is no misfortune for them; pity is for women alone. For women, yes, because with men there is only a lack of love. And, yet, I write this not for women, because their misfortune is sufficiently great that they will find no comfort in the pain of another and it would be unjust of me to wish them to read it. Rather, I strongly suggest that they flee from it and from all things sad, yet even then few will be the days when they can see joy, for such has been ordained by the misfortune into which they have been born. It may have already begun for just one person, but I have no news of him after his misfortune, like mine, bore him away to strange and distant lands and has kept from him any pleasure he might have had, living or dead, as I know so well.

Oh, my dear, true friend, who has taken you away so far from me?*

*For readers well versed in Portuguese literature, this reference to the narrator's "dear, true friend" (and, indeed, the spirit of this entire first section) evokes Portugal's rich medieval tradition of the "Cantiga do Amigo," a popular verse form that was written by a man but from

You and I were wont to share our griefs together (small as they were beside those that were to come later). I told you everything. When you went away, all grew sad and all I could do was look for your return. The loss was even greater because when you left, I was not even given the comfort of knowing in what part of the world you roamed so that I could have lifted up my eyes to see you there. Everything had been taken from me and there was no cure or relief for my ills. To die quickly would have been my greatest wish, but even that was not ordained for me. Although for you, perhaps, there might even have been some vestige of mercy in your misfortune of being taken so far away, for there is no way for you to feel the sorrow of listening to my plaints. But, alas and woe for me, as I go on talking and do not see that the wind is carrying my words away and that the one to whom I am speaking cannot hear them!

I know well that it was not for this that I now wish to write something, for writing calls for great repose and my sorrows lead me back and forth and from one side to another, carrying me along like that, and I am forced to use the words they give me, for they are not constrained so much to serve my skill as they are my grief. Many will be the faults of mine to be found in this little book, but they have been born of my lot. Even if someone finds me full of blame and excuses, the book shall still be just what has been written in it! There is no orderly way to recount sad events because they come about in such a disorderly way. And, also, should no one at all read it, I shall not care, because I am doing it for one person alone, or for no one at all, because, as I have said, I have had no news of him for so long.

---

the perspective of a woman. Importantly, the "Cantiga do Amigo" delivers the woman's heartfelt lament to another woman, to Nature itself, or, via the voice and performance of the troubadour who sings this unique form of "cantiga," to the listener/reader, whose active, imaginative response imparts to the tale being told a complexity and poignancy it would not have otherwise had. The best "Cantigas do Amigo" move their listener/reader from considerations of a specific story of love lost to more existential reflections on the nature of being, of human relationships, and, significantly, on the social and psychological ontology of both women and men. If the content of the "Cantiga do Amigo" cultivates a delicate ambiguity as to the exact nature of the love relationship involved, the style in which it is delivered by the women in question (here, the "moça," or "maiden," of the title and the older, more experienced woman who delivers the "First Dialogue") tends to be singularly frank, spontaneous, and natural.

But if it has been granted, still, that I be rewarded by this small token of my great sighs coming before his eyes, then no matter how many other things I might desire, this would be quite sufficient.

On this mountain, higher than all others, to which I came in search of a solitude different from others and which I found on it, I spent my life as best I could, sometimes going down into the valleys that encircled it, sometimes placing myself on its highest point to look out at the land as it went off to the sea and then to the sea itself as it stretched beyond to end where nobody could see. But when night fell it would take over my thoughts, as I watched the birds seeking out their nests, some calling to each other, wishing, as it would seem, to bring peace upon the land itself, and then, sadly, with my thoughts folded into the ones I had awakened with, I would retire to my poor house, where only God bears good witness to how I slept that night.

That was how I spent my time, when, on one of my walks a while back, as I saw how beautifully morning was raising up and spreading out its grace across the valleys, I left them and went up to higher ground, where the sun, risen now, was taking possession of the knolls and touched their breasts like someone wishing to dominate the land. The gentle birds were flapping their wings and going off in search of one another. The shepherds, playing their pipes in the midst of their flocks, began to appear in the fields. The day seemed to be arriving like that with joy for all. Only my cares — seeing how day was coming on in so powerfully opposite a way from them — withdrew within me, as although all that pleasure and contentment that the day was placing before my eyes was there to be seen, the change had been so great that all that made everything so happy only made me sad. And as my thoughts of what fate had ordained began to enter me, recalling a time that once had been and was never meant to be, these memories dominated me in such a way that I couldn't bear thinking about my home, and I wanted instead to go to some lonely place where I might give vent to my sighs. And the day had barely begun when (seeming to have sensed this) I decided to go to the foot of this mountain, one covered with vast groves and green grasses and with delightful shade. All year long a small river runs here, where I often go to leave my tears and where also countless times I drink them in again, and on quiet nights its tumbling waters give a sad and mournful tone to the heights of this mountain, and which often lulls me to sleep.

Then I would start up again and in my hurry along the path in flight, or from the ill fate that bore me along, I fell three or four times, but so sad was I, that I had nothing more to fear and thus I paid scant heed to what might have been God's trying to tell me of the change that was to come later. When I reached the bank of the river I sought out a shadier spot, but which seemed to lie beyond the stream. I thought then that, because I could not attain what I sought without crossing the waters — which ran quietly there but deeper than in other parts — it occurred to me then that everything I wanted always seemed to require greater effort. As a person who had always avoided anything that might bring me harm, I continued on my way instead, and farther along sat down under the shade of a green ash tree, whose branches reached out over the water where the current was faster but broken by a boulder in the center, splitting the waters into two gushing streams. And as I gazed at it I began to wonder whether events without any understanding might also cause grief in other matters. I began to take some comfort for my hurt because, right there, that boulder was disturbing the water as it wanted to continue on its way, just as my misfortunes in times past had come from my being accustomed to doing everything I wanted most, and now wanting nothing. And I was taken with sadness, because beyond the boulder the water came together again and went its way with no great turmoil, but seemed to be running along even more rapidly than before. And I told myself that it must have to get away as quickly as possible from that boulder, the enemy of its natural course and placed there as if by some force or necessity.

Soon thereafter, as I sat pondering, a nightingale came to light on a green branch that hung over the water and began to sing so sweetly that it captured my ears completely. But as it grew louder with its plaints it seemed to grow weary, wishing to stop, and then it would suddenly start up all over again. All at once that sad little bird complaining there dropped dead into the water, I don't know why, falling through the branches and taking a great many leaves with it — this might have been a sign of mourning by the trees over the bird's disastrous fate. The waters carried it along and the leaves after it. I tried to grab it, but the current there was quite strong and there were bushes growing along the bank, so it was soon out of my sight. But it grieved me ever so much to see something that I had heard singing just a short time before die like that, and it was impossible for me to hold back my tears.

It became clear to me, of course, that I was not weeping like that just over the loss of something in the present, because I had also lost something else in the past. And my thoughts were not entirely off the mark because, although my tears had been caused by the misfortune of that little bird, as they emerged they were joined by others from my sad memories. I sat there like that for a long time, my eyes in the grip of the cares that held them fast even then, and would keep on so doing until the time when a stranger would come, someone whose pitying hands would close these eyes of mine, which never ceased to show me woes.

In that way, staring at where the water was coursing along, I sensed something moving in the forest. Imagining it to be other than a person, I became frightened, but when I glanced over there I saw a woman approaching, and as I took a careful look I saw that she was tall in stature and well-proportioned, with the countenance of a lady, a courtly dame from times gone by. Dressed all in black, with her calm gait and the confident movements of her body, her face and her gaze, she appeared to be someone worthy of respect. Alone she was coming along, and seemingly with such care that she did not have to push aside any branches except when they blocked the way or brushed against her face. Her feet carried her along through the fresh grass and part of her gown extended out over it. Amidst the slow steps she was taking she would from time to time pause and take a weary breath, as though her spirits were about to give out. As she drew closer and caught sight of me, she clutched her hands together, as women do when they are frightened, and remained like that for a moment, as if she had seen something unusual. I was like that, too, not from fear — because her pleasant look made that unnecessary — but from the novelty of seeing something never seen there before although, with my grief, I had been frequenting that place all along the riverbank for a long time.

2. *First Dialogue*

She was soon aware of the state I was also in and spoke, with a pleasant look on her face.

"How wonderful it is," she began, "to find a young maiden here in this wilderness after terrible misfortune had carried off my whole world . . . ," and then, after a pause, her words mingled now with tears, she said, ". . . my son."

Then, drawing a kerchief from her sleeve, she began dabbing her face and came over to where I was sitting. I stood up right away and curtsied, as was called for from the courtesy she had shown me and from her appearance. And she went on.

"How very strange," she said to me, "that after living in this wilderness for such a long time without seeing anyone I meet you, and so, my dear lass, I must know who you are and what you are doing here or what you have come to do, so beautiful and so alone."

It took me some time to reply because of the doubts she had and also the ones I had about what to tell her, but she seemed to understand and said,

"You can tell me everything because I am a woman like you, and from what I can gather from your look, you are very much in the same state as I, because you have a sad regard and your eyes have undone your beauty so much, even though it couldn't be noticed from a distance."

"From a distance, Milady," I replied, "you look to be just what you are when close by. You must not deprive yourself of anything you might find of interest in me, because your attire and all I see in you is filled with sadness — something I have been accustomed to myself for such a long time, and because it has been difficult for me for so long. I do not wish to ask your pity, but I do want to thank you for wishing to know whatever it might be you want while listening for a moment to my ills."

"Do tell me then," she replied, "for staying here and listening to you can also be a new obligation for me, and from your appearance my being obliged to you might also bring me some enjoyment."

For her satisfaction, then, I recounted my story.

"I was a girl who has lived in the wilderness, beyond this riverbank, for a short time only and who will not live for long. I was born in a different land, and different, too, were the many people among whom I grew up. I have fled to this place where there is nothing except the grief I brought along, to this valley where these clear waters you see are flowing, where the dense shadows from the tall groves hang over the green grass and the flowers seem to bloom here at their pleasure. The banks of this cool stream extend all along, and are the sweet dwellings and meeting places for the solitary and delightful birds, and so fitting for my cares, for which, whenever the sun comes out to look after the land, I come this way, because although you see me all alone, I am not. In all the long time I have followed this path, never have I seen anyone but you. The great solitude of this valley and all the land about makes me dare to come this way. You can see quite well that I am not yet a beautiful woman, and since I have no weapons for attack, why should I need any to defend myself? I can go everywhere, safe from everything, except from my grief, for nowhere can I go but that it follows me. A moment ago, I was alone here looking at that boulder (pointing out to her how it sat there hampering the water that wished to continue on its way). Before my eyes, on that branch over it, a nightingale came to perch, singing its sweet song. Every so often there seemed to be another answering from far away. At the height of its song it fell dead like that, into the water, which carried it off so quickly that I was unable to fetch it out. This made me so sad that there came to mind other great disasters of my own that caused me, too, to be carried away from where I could no longer return."

With these words my eyes flooded with tears and I brought my hands up to them.

"This, Milady, is what I was doing when you appeared and I am always like this, weeping or on the verge of tears."

I had replied, but I was holding myself back a little because how could I ask something similar of her, something that had been the cause of her tears, for it had taken her so long to say just ". . . son," and I thought that perhaps she didn't wish to say anything more.

"But it is obvious, my dear, that you are not of this place and have not been here long, but of the disasters that take place along this bank and that might frighten you, one is a story that is much spoken of hereabouts and in all the land, one that took place a long time ago. I remember my father telling it as a tale when I was a young girl. I think about it still —

now because of the great unhappy events in it — and even though some-one else's ills cannot comfort those of another, it has been of some help for my suffering to know that this is an old story where things happen without any reason and against all reason. Since it appears that you have not yet heard it, I shall be glad to tell it to you because, as I understand from what you have told me, sad things can be pleasing."

I answered, "The sun is high and I should like very much to hear it, hear it from you. Know then that it was not by chance that I sought this place out for my woes as it has been accustomed to their like for such a long time. There is something else I should like to ask you first, Milady, but let it wait for later, because there will be time enough for everything, for even though the story is about miseries, as you say, it still cannot take so short a time as the day itself."

"The days are long now," she replied, "they can never be so short that I cannot fulfill your wants as best I can. This is a simple gift from me to you. But what was it you wished first?"

"Something that need not cause you any concern now," I replied. "It cannot be of any great matter for you to wish to hear it, what I wanted before, or after, or never, I just want it to come. Do not take this to mean that I should not like to hear the story, because it is not out of sadness that I find the time short now. I am quite ready. Recount it, therefore, Milady, recount it because it is sad and we shall enjoy our time with what was not made for you or me."

"Pity me," she began, "because I only make myself sadder by seeking out the misfortunes of others — as if my own were not enough — and so many times in these lonely places I go about frightening myself as though they were still happening to me! So do not think that some distant grief does not seem that way in the present, because the long-enduring pain my body has suffered has made it so accustomed to bearing it that the poor thing lives within it, and this is how it has been with me. It is one of the great complaints I have of the body, that there is nothing that it will not become accustomed to over a long time. And so it has been for many years, as I do not live for myself, and come to this deserted place, fleeing people who only see me get up in the morning and go to bed at night. I am so pleased to find you, too, an intimate of grief, so that we can console each other's disconsolate state, just as a person ill from poison cures herself with a different one. When I first saw you, away from all the people in this land for so long a time, and I discerned something in all that time to talk about, I was disturbed. But it was not so much my seeing you as talking to you afterwards, and now the more I look at you the more I want to look. Your words tell me now that your heart must be sorely tried. From the marks the tears have left on your face (which does not seem given to bear these sorrows), I understand how much you have been taken over by your cares, which do not seem to be baseless. I see you as a young maiden with a life still to live in this world. Cursed by the misfortune that began so early for you and the one which, so late, has yet to end for me!

"It would please me very much if you were to tell me more about your troubles, piece by piece, for, as I have heard it from you, it has only made me all the sadder. But if that is how you wish it, my lass, I am content and I bow to your will, for if you cannot avoid misfortune it often bodes best to keep it under cover. And yet, as pain, it might still bear some good, for even if it cannot help lessen the hurt, it might make it easier to bear. This is enough for women's griefs, because we do not have a cure for ills as men do; for in the short span of my life I have learned that men have no griefs, only women grieve. We women are sad because when sadness saw that men move from one thing to another — and since most things, with continuous change, either scatter or are lost — and with all the things that keep men busy all the time, sadness turned its burdens over to us, the poor women, either because we hate changes or because we have no place to which we can flee. So no matter how unjust and serious misfortunes may be, when they come to men these creatures cannot do anything about them and turn them over to us, the weaker partners. Thus it is that we suffer a double ill, one that we suffer ourselves and one that was not made for us. Men think about other things (and women's matters do not concern them), men are long accustomed to their concerns and they have scant consideration for our griefs. Whether women therefore have good reason to be sadder or not can be known only by someone who knows what a sorrow it is to keep the truth unknown."

At this I couldn't hold back a weary sigh that came from deep within my soul. And as she sensed my trying to hide it, she reached out her right hand and took mine, suspecting my pretense, and spoke to me again.

"When I was your age I was living in my father's house. On those long and fearsome winter nights I would sit sewing among the other women of the house, but I would usually keep to myself. In order to ease the work, we would have one of the women tell a tale so that the evening would not seem so long. But the lady of the house, old now and who had seen much and heard many things from being so old, always said that a task of that nature should belong to her alone. Then she would go on to narrate tales of knight errantry. And in all truth, the affronts and great misfortunes that the knights became involved in because of fair maidens led me to feel sorry for them. And I thought about how a knight, resolutely armed and mounted on his fine steed, as he passed along the banks of a river in the delightful countryside, might be just as sad as a tender maid in her high quarters or on her balcony or shut up behind walls could be, seeing herself enclosed, a creature of such scant strength guarded by so many things. In order to restrain her wishes, great defenses had been set up, but with chinks that nevertheless let small annoyances creep in. Knights had more ways in which to express their griefs and maidens fewer, which made them seem sadder than the men. If after discovering so many things I could have turned back, I might have borne less grief for some of the things that have made me grieve, because we must expect some hope from all that pain. A woman should not have it any other way, or at least pretend she would not.

"I say this, my dear, because from back there when your heart gave out with a sigh and you tried to hide it as best you could, I surmise that because of some great injustice your feelings have been terribly saddened, because a person of your age is not meant for wild places like this. Even if men had never become accustomed to their aggravation of maidens, it would still be the cause of great sorrow, but with things as they are, who is not to be aggravated? I could go on for a long time telling you things like this — even though our acquaintance has been brief — because I am older than you and because it is the truth, and so there is no reason to spend as much time on it as on other matters. How many maidens has the land already devoured because of the longings left them by knights whom other lands have devoured along with other longings? Books are filled with the stories of maidens left weeping by knights who rode off, but who nevertheless still had to spur on their horses because those knights were not as unloving as they might have seemed.

"In this tale there will only be the two friends about whom the story I promised you is concerned. In them alone, I think, exists the faithfulness that had been lost in others, and I also think that because of this, other men were ordered to kill them treacherously, with no thought of the evil entailed therein. Because not only does evil hate good, it does not even want good remembered. When my father told about the villainy in the way in which the false knights killed the two friends, he said that he wished he had never heard about it or known of it because, in the short time left him to live, he could see how the generation of evil was still hereabouts. But if sorrow for the death of the pair was great, how much greater was the sorrow over the death of the two maidens whom evil fate had brought to such a state, because not only had it brought the pair of young worthies to die for them, it also brought death to them as well. What the two friends had done for the women and for themselves was the pledge they were obliged to fulfill according to the knighthood they professed. The women also fulfilled, along with them, a pledge that I hold in the highest esteem — for they would not have done so on behalf of any other men — whereas the men, because of their code of chivalry, would have been obliged to do the same for other damsels in distress. Thus, for those who have done their utmost, one must weep the utmost at their deaths. And yet, for my part, I grieve for them equally, the ones because they were women and the others because they were unlike other men. I say that between us, because my son was also a man."

With that word the tears began to run down her face and, unable to stop, her voice, catching in her throat, went on.

"You must pardon me, my dear — because at my age I might well call you daughter — if you see me do this so many times, because tears should be no strangers to you as you have had such a great urge to seek out lonely places like this, where we are. In other times they say this place belonged to many noble knights and beautiful maidens, and even now where shepherd boys watch their flocks they come across weapons and jewels of great value, all of which would seem to give this valley a sadder shade than any other. I do not know how this world became so overturned. There used to be many people in these valleys that now lay deserted. People used to stroll through them where now wild beasts roam. Some abandoned what others took over. Why was there so much change in just one land? And yet it seems that the land itself has also changed along with everything on it, and this is because the time when it was happy has passed. I can see how, from when it was ennobled by many people and fine buildings, and was not yet a sad place, it has become these deep woods, which nature has brought forth. Still, here and there in this valley are some few ancient trees that, with the long passage of time and their lack of proper care — given the uses for which they had been planted — seem to bear a different foliage from what they once did when, with the helping hands of orchard- men, they produced their perfect fruit. Everything in this valley is filled with sad memories for someone who has heard tell of what they say hap- pened here in times long gone by, and which seems so unlikely from how the place is today.

"But everything is like that, after all. Some things are done in the place of others as if they were not to be done. Little did the two friends think, when they accepted the high task of watching over matters in this valley simply to please the two lovely maidens, that it would end in the displea- sure of these. And little did the maidens think, as they dressed and richly prepared themselves to see the two knight friends on that day of great misfortune, that they would never see them again. Our fate, from some whim, I know not which, lays things out before us and yet we cannot see them. Everything changes in a way we cannot understand and so grief comes over us when we are least prepared for it, because we suffer at the same time for the good we have lost and for the evil we can acquire."

Here she gave a great sigh, as if she wished to tell more, and she went on.

"But now it is time for me to carry out what I promised you, for I can see quite clearly that my grief has swept me away."

the Tale of
LAMENTOR & BELISA

They tell the tale that long ago a noble knight of great renown came from foreign lands and made landfall close to where the small river running here enters the sea. He came in a great ship bearing a rich cargo and also two beautiful sisters, one of whom was dearer to him than the other. So that she would feel less longing for her native soil, he brought along her sister, a younger damsel than the one on whose account he had come in search of foreign lands. It was said that they were the daughters of a man of very high station, as was later learned from the many knights errant who roamed about the world in those times — that is too long a story, however.

After landing, Lamentor (for that was the name he was known by in these parts) — arriving in the way he did and having full knowledge of the land and its inhabitants — had no wish to settle down anywhere near many people, and one morning left the ship and, after his servants had made all the necessary preparations, taking all his goods, he set out up through this valley. The two sisters traveled in elegant sedan chairs that Lamentor had brought from the ship, the older sister being in an advanced state of pregnancy. It was a lovely morning, just as if it had been arranged that way so that the land might bring them more contentment. It was the month of April, that time of year when the trees burst into bloom and the birds, silent until then, begin to renew their plaints of the year before. Passing through the woods along this valley — which were much the same as they are now — they took pleasure in one thing and another as Lamentor sought every way possible for his lady and the maid who was her sister to overcome both the longing for their land and the lingering effects of their sea voyage. But when they came to a bridge (which is still there), planning to cross over it, a squire was standing before it and he addressed Lamentor thus,

"Sir knight, if you wish to pass over you must do one of two things:

either confess that the knight who guards this bridge does so with more right than anyone else or let a joust decide."

"In order to give a proper answer to that question, there are many things one would have to know," Lamentor replied. "How is one to know if there is reason for him to favor someone without first knowing who he is and what it is he wishes? But I cannot deal with that right now, and it is sufficient merely to follow my own wishes rather than what he or the whole world might want. What I am certain of is this: I should like to know more about him and his reasons for guarding this bridge, and for his keeping those reasons to himself, even though they be the greatest in the world for him. You must tell him, my good squire, that he would do well to let me pass rather than let a joust be the judge."

The squire, who had already seen the sedan chairs and thought that he had never seen anything so beautiful, replied:

"Such a mission would be of no use because he is so prideful that no one can bargain with him, and there is also a good reason, for one week from today he will have maintained this challenge for three years without ever finding a knight who could best him — the list of all there are in this land is long. Also, the appointed time was set out for him by a maiden, the most beautiful in all these parts as has ever been known till now. She is the daughter of the lord of the castle that stands up on that height, and she promised the knight her love if he guarded this bridge under the conditions that you have just heard. And yet, sir knight, if he were to know of the company you have with you, he would have good reason to fear now more than ever. And yet I cannot tell him that, because I have brought him such messages at other times, thinking I was doing the right thing, and his response was rather nasty. And afterwards, should the matter turn out other than we both desired, he would trounce me as though my good intentions had been to blame for the outcome."

"In that case, then, bring on the joust," said Lamentor, glancing over at the chairs.

The squire then raised a bugle that he had tied around his neck by a cord and blew a call, whereupon a well-armed knight on horseback emerged from a thick wood beyond the bridge. He rode straight to the bridge and they both fell to jousting immediately. My father recounted many details of their great efforts and valor, which I shall not relate to you — for while we women do greatly enjoy hearing about knightly deeds, it is not proper for me to recount such things nor do they seem the same as when men relate them. I will tell you about it, however, if I can remember everything. What I do recall is that my father spoke of how they broke lances three times and on the fourth, the knight of the bridge fell, and from the great fall brought on by that great clash, he lay there unable to raise himself. Lamentor dismounted quickly, and when he reached him he found him unable to speak. When his visor was lifted the knight looked to be mortally wounded. He regained consciousness in a short time, however, and with his color all changed he lifted his eyes to Lamentor, who was leaning over him, and said:

"Alas, sir knight, God has made his test, and it was something that you have never seen, or what at least you will never see again."

Lamentor felt great pity for him, especially when he saw the tears running down his face. Taking him by the arm and helping him up, he told him:

"Of love, sir knight, you have good reason for complaint, for just as it made you guard this crossing, so, too, it brought me to cause you trouble. It grieves me, as a man, for having done this to you, and it also grieves me that I came to do it because I was a lover. If I can make amends for this in any way that suits your pleasure, please tell me what that might be."

The knight of the bridge, seeing how courteous Lamentor was, felt that there was every reason to thank him for that wish, but he had such pain in his heart that he could not bring himself to accept it. But since he was of good breeding, he said:

"Overweening love has no place in reason's realm." And then, as if excusing himself, he added, "But I shall be avenged on other women, far from this land here, where my eyes must not see anything upon which they have been cast. But this vengeance will weigh heavily on me because it can only be on my part and for me alone."

Speaking thus he turned away and began walking up the valley, but, badly injured by the great fall he had taken, and from which there seemed to be something broken inside, he did not go far. His squire had taken care of his horse and was starting out after his master when he came upon him lying face down on the ground. He ran over to help him up, but when he saw that the knight was in a mortal condition he began to wail and moan. Lamentor, hearing him, rode over. Finding the squire holding his dying master in his arms, he dismounted quickly and joined him, seeing how the knight was losing consciousness and in the final moments of his life.

"What is this, sir knight?" Lamentor asked him. "Try hard! Is this true to the oath you took to the order of knighthood?"

And upon hearing these words, the knight looked at Lamentor and slowly reached out his right hand to him in, as it seemed, a gesture of peace, and with a weary voice told him:

"If I had the strength I would forgive everything, but it fails me now just when it means so much for me to live."

From the effort he had made to say this, like a man suffering from some great inner pain, he lost his breath, closing his eyes and lying there like someone who had left this world. A moment later, he opened them again and made a motion with his face to where stood the castle of the maiden for whom he was guarding the crossing, with its view of the entire valley. And as he raised his eyes in that direction he seemed to be remembering that only eight days had remained to fulfill the task assigned him, something that grieved him above all else as he muttered these last words:

"Oh, castle, how close to you I was just now!"

And with that he let his eyes close wearily forever.

The two sisters had come over now, in their chairs, along with everyone else. When they saw by the face of the knight of the bridge how handsome and still quite young he was, they all grew rather sad over such a great disaster. Lamentor, seeing how the squire had thrown himself at the feet of his master sobbing, took pity on him (for in their conversation at the bridge he had taken him to be a person of good manners and breeding), and he went over to console him, drawing him away from where he was weeping and telling him:

"Temperance is most praiseworthy in things that matter, and since weeping is of no avail, moderation is called for all the more, unless tears are unavoidable. Your master died as a knight and therefore I say to you and all who loved him that you should not be sad, rather you should be happy that he had such great courage that he could not bear defeat. All things depend on fate."

"This misfortune belongs to me alone," the squire said, weeping, "because I have been left behind. This grieves me not so much as how it was brought on and the one who caused it to be so."

"The love of a knight," replied Lamentor, wishing to learn the cause of it all, "makes a good thing of whatever he might do."

"Only in cases where it is a thankful thing," said the squire, "but my master loved a maiden whose only weapon against him was her beauty and whose desire was not for him, although he loved her more than anything in the world. People in her household said that on the day she agreed to the arrangement she fell to tearful weeping, for the only reason she had agreed was that her father had been quite taken with my master, and his strong arguments, even at the time of his death, had won his daughter's agreement."

They were all startled to hear this because the knight of the bridge was handsome and had fought valiantly in the encounter. Lamentor, on whom this weighed heavily because of the great efforts he had seen his opponent put into the contest, said sadly:

"Console yourself, for love never forgives a lack of it. Sooner or later you will see vengeance."

The squire threw himself at his master's feet again and said:

"Sir knight, for death there is no vengeance."

Lamentor lifted him up again and told him that there would be time for weeping, but that right now he must try to decide what was to be done. The squire replied that he would leave there on a day's journey to where his master had his castle. There, was a widowed sister — to whom he had turned over his feudal estates so that she would have something to live on while he was off on his adventures — and a party would come from there to bear his master to the resting-place of his ancestors, for she loved him very much. He asked Lamentor to leave one of his squires to look after his master's body.

The sun was sinking now and it was time to rest and dine, most especially because they had just come off the sea. Not far from where they were by the bridge was a delightful place to take their ease, with a grove that had a stream running through it. Lamentor had planned for them to dine there, and that was what he set out to do. He told the squire that they wished to rest in that place, and that he would give him one of the litters on which to bear his master, and if there was anything else to be done, he would do it gladly. The squire thanked him, saying that was agreeable, and began putting things in order. It happened then that the sister of the knight of the bridge — knowing that there was only a week remaining of the pledge, and with the great love she bore him — had decided the day before to make all the preparations and come to that place. She wished to be with him at the end of the obligation he had made for love, and she was certain that he would complete the term with great honor as he had now maintained his stand with no knight in all those parts having passed through. But when she arrived and saw everyone and also the litters, she was at a loss for words. Stiffening when she saw the squire — whom she knew well — going about sobbing, she asked him what was wrong and then looked over and saw her brother lying on the fine spreads that Lamentor had ordered laid out. She quickly dismounted and ran over. Casting her wig onto the ground, she began to loosen her long hair over where her brother's body lay, saying:

"There are no rules where there is great grief."

This she said because in that land there was a custom left over from earlier times that was stringently observed and which forbade a woman, under severe penalty, to appear with her head uncovered except in the presence of her husband. She reached over and kept hugging and kissing him, saying:

"Oh, brother of mine, what kind of death is this that has carried you off unable to speak to me? An evil fate has deceived me and brought me from your castle. The turn of fate you had taken to be so promising before you left on this adventure made me leave home to see you, and now we have seen nothing of what we had hoped to see. How sad am I, the one you ran to embrace, saying 'Three years hence, sister of mine, you shall see what I have hoped for most in all the world and the one, begging your forgiveness, I love the most.' It immediately struck my heart and I said to you, 'The term is long for the one accepting it, but seems less so for the one who sets it.' But you, wishing for this reward, had no ears for me. 'A great love demands a great proof,' was your reply, and the evil of it has been many times over great, but the earth shall not devour me with this grief until I have done all in my power to see that the one who has cost you and me so dearly pays for that long term!"

The two sisters, who had now decided to leave their sedan chairs, went over to her and, since they did not know the language of the land, holding her between them, began to caress her in an attempt at consolation. But she, weeping, said in a strong voice:

"Leave me to weep, ladies, for my brother has no one else to weep for him."

Lamentor, who had traveled far and wide and did know the language, came over and told her:

"Knights, Milady, give their lives in feats of arms, as your brother did, and they should not be wept over like other men, for they have found what they sought. You, Milady, although you have good reason to be sad for what you have lost, the finest knight in all this land, also have good reason to praise God for making him that. Leave off weeping and look to what must be done while you still have him with you, because it would be scandalous if you were to be thinking more about your grief than about your brother."

Thereupon he called over the squire and told him what he had already arranged. She took this to be good and went along. They laid the knight of the bridge in a sedan chair, wrapped in the fine cloths, and the sister wept as she asked to be put in with him. Lamentor took her by one arm and her maid by the other, as the sister was unable to get in by herself, and they placed her inside. As Lamentor untied the curtains of the litter and drew them together as a sign of mourning, he leaned over to her and said:

"Although this may not be the time for it, Milady, since I do not know when I shall see you again, please know that I am at your service. You may learn the rest from the squire."

She gave no reply, all covered up as she was and leaning over her brother's face. Lamentor dropped the curtains and they went on their way.

Everyone was saddened by that misfortune, but Lamentor, as he wiped away the tears that her departure had brought on, did not forget the ones he was traveling with and went over to where his wife and her sister were, telling them:

"We can leave now, ladies, because we have no more part in the shrouding of others."

Taking his wife by the hand, he ordered his people to set out for the place he had chosen before, telling them what they were to do there. In the meantime all three went over to the riverbank hereabouts, gazing at it and talking of many things. They stayed like that only for a while because all that had to be done was the pitching of a sumptuous tent and then, because they were also traveling with abundant supplies, they would be well taken care of. They rested for quite some time, awaiting the return of the litter, but as it became too late to travel on, they remained there also for that night, which fate had now ordained to be forever. Belisa (for that was the name of the lady who was pregnant) fell asleep there as they waited for the litter. And when she awoke, somewhat upset, she found Lamentor putting his loving arms around her.

"Not now," she told him.

From the upset with which she had awakened, he could see that she had been dreaming, and he asked her what was wrong.

"I was dreaming," she replied, "that you and I had been tied together with a cord, that I cut it, and you never came back."

Lamentor felt those words pierce his heart, as they ultimately would, and the presentiment saddened him greatly, as though his soul were foretelling some evil for him and he was unable to pretend otherwise, which she noticed and asked him:

"What's wrong? Has what I told you brought on this change in you?"

Moving the conversation toward something that might bring on a change in her, too, and to put the dangers of her pregnancy out of her mind, he replied:

"I must confess to you, my dear, even though I am forced into it by my feeling now, that I do not wish to think or talk about it. It made me melancholy, and you must forgive me because it could not have been from you, since dreams come from the fantasy we carry inside. And so it appeared that you meant with your dream that you would see me no more because you did not trust my love for you, or did not trust me, certain as you are of one or the other or both."

And she gave way to great laughter, enough to rid him of what he might have been thinking, as she came over to tell him:

"You have traveled long and far to discover that mistrust! I forgive you because this day has been quite ill-fated enough, with all the terrible things that have happened."

They spent there the remains of that day and its sunlight, which would set on more troubles than it had dawned upon, and about which you shall hear.

After nightfall, everyone having retired, Belisa began to feel a slight discomfort, but as the pains were growing stronger, she went to call her sister. Awakening her as she slept on a nearby cot, Belisa told her how the pains were increasing. Lady Aónia (for that was the sister's name) then awakened the women of the household, including one who knew much about midwifery — for which reason Lamentor had brought her along, because when they left Belisa was pregnant, and had it been possible to disguise her state, he would not have brought her to strange lands that way, but in youthful days there is no better remedy for love than exile. Belisa, who loved Lamentor more than anything else in the world, asked the other women to help her out of the bed where she was lying and over to her sister's cot. She did not wish to awaken him, tired as he was from all the traveling and quite in need of rest. This was done as quietly as possible. The women spent the rest of the night watching over Belisa's pains, but Lady Aónia, who saw her sister's troubles growing worse, asked:

"Milady sister, do you wish me to call my dear brother?"

"No, in the name of pity," she replied, "do not call him. It will please God to make this pain go away and we can spare him that at least."

"It will please God," said the midwife from where she stood, "for there seems to be no sign of birth as I can see, Milady. It's too soon. It must be because of the trip or being in a different place."

But as the morning came on there was no lessening of the pains; indeed, they seemed to be growing stronger. Belisa began to have seizures, as if her heart were stopping, but she was able to bear the first one, and the next one, too. When the third one came, however, it was so great that it affected her ability to speak somewhat, and when she recovered she looked at her sister and said:

"I think you should call him now."

But as she began to feel better then, she turned back to her sister, who was about to call him, saying:

"No, don't call him. I seem to be feeling better."

Belisa lay exhausted for a long time, and as the rich robe she was wearing was all stained from the remedies they had placed over her heart, she turned to the women and said:

"Dress me in a different robe. If I am to die, I don't wish to be looking like this, at least."* When she heard those words the Lady Aónia began to weep, and when she looked at Belisa she saw tears in her eyes, too, as she attempted to say something, but the pain would not let her, as it became more intense than before. The midwife, who saw how exhausted she was, said that it would be best to stand her up on her feet, and as her sister moved to hold on one side of her, Belisa turned to her and said:

"I don't know what this could be."

But the stabs of pain were so great then, and coming so rapidly, that it was no use to stand her completely up, so they placed her in a kind of sitting position, but finally the misery was such that she soon went into her death throes and her speech began to falter. Lifting her eyes to her sister she managed to say:

"Get him! Get him!"

Lady Aónia, immediately ran to call Lamentor, weeping as she went. He was in a deep sleep and she told him,

"Wake up, sir! Wake up! Belisa is being taken away from you!"

Lamentor stood up at once and reached for the short sword he kept by the head of his bed. But when he saw them all weeping around Aónia's bed and Belisa, who had risen part way, already half gone from this world, he ran to embrace her, asking:

"What is it, Milady?"

And with those words the tears began to run down his face and hers. Belisa then lifted a sleeve of her robe to wipe away his tears, but she was unable to continue and she let her arm drop and then, fixing her eyes on him, she said, "Forever . . . never more." She closed them slowly then, as if under the heavy weight of leaving him like that.

Lamentor, unable to bear it, fell down in turn as though dead and remained that way for a long time. Just then the midwife heard a baby's cry coming from the bed and, guessing what it meant, went over and discovered a newborn little girl. Weeping heavily, she took it in her arms, and with her eyes still moist spoke to it thus:

---

*This reference to funeral attire, rites, and ceremonies of mourning, applicable to both the Christian and Jewish traditions, can be taken (as can many other aspects of the text) as an indication of the author's likely Jewish heritage.

"You poor little thing, a girl born as your mother wept! How shall I raise you, a foreign child in a foreign land? Cursed was the day we left the sea to have this storm on land!"

But, with her wisdom, she worked at caring for her, taking it all into her own hands, for Lamentor and the sister had a heavier task before them. So she arranged all that had to be done and saw to everything.

Milady Aónia, remembering what the widowed lady had done over the body of her dead brother and how proper a custom at a time of mourning it seemed then, even though it was not followed in her country, loosened the braids of her wonderfully long hair and covered her sister and Lamentor, for she really thought he was also dead because of the great love he bore her sister and the way he looked. Then, in her extreme fatigue, she began to say aloud:

"Woe is me, a maiden with so little time left her, unsheltered in a foreign land, without any kin, without anyone, without any happiness! For you, my dear sister, have left me alone like this, so far away, and in such a place as this. You asked me to come with you so you would not be lonely and now that same thing has befallen me. Oh, unlucky me! My mother brought me up for a different kind of future. She was mistaken, and now I am paying for her mistake. A great injustice, sir knight, had been done me before your eyes. Of the many women you have protected I am the only one who was not. Woe is me, what shall I do, where shall I go?"

And she threw herself over her sister's body, but when she mentioned the knight, he awoke as though out of a dream and saw all the grief and tears that lay before him. He was speechless, but seeing how the Lady Aónia was mistreating herself, he made an effort and went over to stop her from so cruelly punishing herself, saying:

"Courage, Milady. Fortune has called upon someone just as disconsolate to console you."

Then he went to raise her up, but when he tried to speak to her he lost his voice. There stood the two of them, sadly moaning and passing on a word or two of grief to one another, words begun in their sorrow, but broken with their sobs.

The Tale of
BINMARDER & AÓNIA

✳ ✳ ✳
✳ ✳
✳

It was already morning bright when a knight chanced to arrive at the bridge. He came from distant lands in search of adventure and had been sent by a lady who loved him and to whom he owed more than his love alone. Finding nobody at the bridge, and with the sound of such heavy weeping nearby, he sensed some great mystery and some matter of great sorrow. He set out to where it was coming from and came upon a splendid tent with great weeping, both inside and out. Inquiring of a servant there what might be the cause of it all, the servant told him. Dismounting then he sent one of Lamentor's squires in ahead of him and slowly entered. As he did so he caught sight of the Lady Aónia, so beautiful with her hair hanging loosely over her face, some strands all wet with tears revealing her countenance. He was immediately carried away with love for her—no one else being there to take the part of his other love—and since this love came to him along with pity, it was as if the other one did not exist. Now, in the presence of the Lady Aónia, he was led to forget his other love (except for regrets at having spent so much time in doing her bidding). That was how he was seized with great love for the Lady Aónia, and later we shall see how he was to die for her—he was one of the two friends about whom this story was told. That was why my father would say that this knight's love would bring him death from the very passion that had raised him so high, but that we shall hear in its own good time.

Lamentor had now asked the knight to enter, but he did not see him until the knight was standing by his side with words of consolation. Lamentor accepted them as best he could, but did not linger over them as he was so little disposed to do so. After they had remained like that for some time, and Lamentor saw that the knight had made no mention of taking his leave, he spoke to him with some urgency.

"Sir knight, I am grateful for your visit and may it please God that on another and happier occasion I shall be able to repay you, but we are traveling and, as you can see, our accommodations are only what you have before your eyes. This is the only abode we have for our grief. You, sir, must be on your way and not partake in so much sorrow, for the sorrow of others also offers grief to those who see it. You must excuse me now, but at the moment there is no way in which I can be of service for your wishes."

The knight turned his eyes toward Lady Aónia and said, "I have nowhere to go from here," and the tears that fell onto his chest seemed to suggest that he would be leaving his heart behind, but seeing that there was only that tent and another smaller one besides in that place, it was clear that there was no room for strangers, even though he did not feel he was one in his heart. So when he arose he spoke again.

"Wherever I go I shall share no small part of this grief of yours, sir. I should be quite willing to help you see it through. But as it stands you are a knight, sir, and, also, you have come from distant lands, as one of your retinue has told me. Thus it is, that this cannot be the first sorrow you have seen, for even in one's very own lands those who have never left them are still not free of sorrows every day, and every hour of those days."

And repeating that he was prepared to help in whatever way was wished of him, he took his leave, his eyes still set on the Lady Aónia as the tent flap soon cut off his view. When he turned away completely, it was as though he had to tear his eyes away from there. That was how he left the tent, and we shall leave him for later.

Lamentor returned to his weeping, as he had good reason for it. As he and the sister remained that way for a long time and as the sun was now climbing up to midday, the midwife, who from here on shall be called the Nurse, charged as she was with the care of the infant girl and wise as she was and with many years of experience, came over to where they were all caught up in their weeping, and said,

"Milord and Milady, you still have much time left you, for misfortune is the same in this land as it is in our own. Leave off your tears, then, for this is no time for you not to look knightly, sir, nor for you, Milady, to look womanly. You must remember that this grief belongs to us all, and ours is just as great for not only must we bear it but we must console others, too. Since we shall bear this sorrow always, let those of us who are alive make an effort at least. The dead are owed their burial and there are things that must be done. Let us see to this last gift which the living can give them. Here we have the body of the Lady Belisa above ground and it seems most proper for us to lend an effort in the lesser part of her departure lest she be upset by our denying her what belongs to her, as there is nothing more that she can ask of us."

With those words, which had been spoken with tears and great sorrow on the part of everyone, she helped the Lady Aónia to rise by holding her arm, and she led her to the small tent where the body had been laid out. Then she came back for Lamentor and helped him there, too. After that she went about arranging what had to be done. Lamentor did not wish to bear Belisa's body to any other place. Rather, he ordered that where she died would be her grave, and it was his decision that never, as long as he lived, would he move from that place. And so it was.

In the land whence they had come it was the custom, before the dead were buried, for the closest kin to come and kiss them on the cheeks, with the nearest relative being the last, and for members of the household to kiss them on the feet. It was carried out like a greeting or a leave-taking, as might have been done in happier times. When everything had been prepared, the Nurse went to call Lamentor and the Lady Aónia. When Aónia leaned over to kiss her sister's cheeks, she stiffened and spoke these words,

"In a different land there would have been more people come to do this than here in this land!"

Then she started to scratch at her own beautiful face, and a sad wailing arose from all there at that sight, all remembering their own grief and drawing near, then, to kiss Belisa's feet. Lamentor, grieving now more than he had ever done, tearing many sighs from his soul, followed custom and said,

"Alas, Milady Belisa, how can I make my tribute to you? You left your land for me, for me you left your mother! Who was it that took you from me in foreign lands to sadden me so? Some great evil must have been envious of me, for you had made me the most fortunate knight in all the world and now this has left me the most distressed. Oh, unfortunate knight who for you, Milady, was rewarded with a grave in an alien land, two of them for my life: yours shall hold your body but mine both my body and my soul. Was not the cord that joined us tight enough, Milady? How could you have cut it without me? Did you not remember that it would be I who was left to be no more without you? You charged them, I am told, that they should not awaken me and for them to take care of me. It was not enough that my misfortune should be the worst in the world, but that it should come to me in the worst way, as someone else was pulling you away from me. I wanted only to see you, and even then you were grieving for me, wishing to wipe away my tears and my unhappiness. Your hand then failed you as you ceased to be the mistress of your wishes, and the last look you gave me showed that along with your will your soul was also departing. I owe more years yet before I follow upon your path, but I owe my sorrows more, so I shall stay behind here with them, the better to remain here without you."

So saying he fulfilled the custom. And as the Nurse saw then that she was the only one to take up the burden of the last rites, she led Lamentor and Lady Aónia over and she laid a splendid cloth over Belisa's face and said,

"Now it is the time for you to gaze upon heaven, where you have the good fortune to be, for here is the earth. Anyone who loves it after having left it, no matter how great the love, will be wrong."

These words might have been of great consolation had it been possible for that grief to be consoled. And that was how she was buried.

Let us leave the deeds of Lamentor for now, many as they were and which he performed for his great love of Belisa, because as this tale is about the two friends, I dislike making it longer because there is much to tell about them. Let the deeds await some other moment in time.

Thus I return to the knight who had left the tent. So distressed was he that he was unable to go very far, so he dismounted and sat down at the foot of an ash tree, there near the riverbank and the bridge. In order to think things through more calmly, he had his squire take his horse away to graze along the bank, for he feared that if his man saw him like this it might engender some suspicion in him and he would go tell Aquelísia (the one for whose sake he had come there, as you have heard). She had only wanted the best from him, and he had been unable to show it thus far by his deeds, because people would come to her bearing tales of everything he was doing, so that what he considered to be good would sometimes seem to be bad—and he could not prevent them from seeming so either, something that would in the end make it sad for her—and with the great love she had for him, this would sadden her, too.

As the knight sat under the ash tree he was a long time turning many scraps of fantasy over in his mind, which, as he remembered that Aquelísia loved him, made it seem wrong for him to have left her. On the other hand, as he recalled how fine Aónia had appeared to him, it seemed an affront to love itself not to be in love with her. Beauty and obligation thus held him trapped between them, waiting to see which one would carry him off. In the end the one closer by had more power. My father would say that obligation lost because its payment did not lead directly to love and that beauty conquered because it was something that was paid on sight. One of two daughters of great beauty, whose mother loved them more than she did herself, Aquelísia obliged this knight to promise so many deeds that she enwrapped him completely in these duties, leaving nothing to be owed to beauty. She seemed to love him so much that she could not bear any delay and she laid everything upon him at once, with no chance for him to do things gradually. That was how she gave him great obligations, but she had also given him great love.

Pity the poor maiden who thinks that deeds will make men fall in love with her, as if this were the way to bring out love. It is quite the opposite, for men fall in love after the presumptuous disdain that follows gentle looks or the difficulties of their deeds. It must come from instinct for this not to matter much, while their chores do matter much indeed. We women are different, gentle by nature, and we act otherwise. When men judge us, however, what reasons can they give, for what else is love if not instinctive? It cannot be given or taken by force. Whether it be for the bad fortune of women or the good luck of men, good deeds can catch the former and disdain the latter. This will be the only way by which they can fall in love, unless they are there already. So who will set the rules of love? And yet this displeasure, which is its true name, has brought so many to an unfortunate end, as you will see in the matter of this knight about whom I am telling. Not in vain did Aquelísia lift her hands to heaven and ask for vengeance upon him.

Nevertheless, in the end he decided to abandon her because he thought that Lady Aónia was the most beautiful creature he had ever seen, and he also thought that as she had come from distant lands and was a stranger in this one, she was more in need of his love. This hope, even though he could see that it was a quite distant one, was yet of great help in confirming or increasing the love he had for her, which is much the same as when something has blocked the sun and, if it is complete, the shadow cast is much greater than the blockage that has brought it about. That is how it is with people in love, small as their hopes may be, they are always fully upheld and thus much larger than the barriers that have cut off the desired object, making that love all the greater. Because of this, there will later on be born thoughts of death or great sadness, which will come to dominate. It came to be that way with this knight, as he could think of nothing else but how to separate from his squire without letting the break arouse any suspicions on the latter's part, for his greatest wish was to enjoy that place. This was important because he knew how greatly it would hurt the squire to see him abandon Aquelísia, for the squire was of her household and she had given him orders to accompany the knight. She told him only that she was to be taken in marriage by the knight, and since she was high-born and would inherit great estates, this would allow him to give up the practice of arms with honor.

Finally, following carefully the plans he had decided upon, he called the squire to him and gave him a long list of reasons, among which he said that he did not think it well that he himself should be the one to bear to Milady Aquelísia news of adventures he had yet to encounter, as this would not be proper, given the love he had for her. The knight further told the squire that owing to his lack of good fortune someone else should be the bearer of such news, because he could not appear before her with it. He would await his return in the castle nearby instead, expecting a message that would set him off on another adventure, since the one he had set out upon could not be fulfilled.

After the squire had left — deceived as would also be the one to whom he was bearing the message — the knight was left alone, and he gave some thought to changing his name so that neither his whereabouts nor where he was going would be known. Love had conquered him so completely that he now wished to leave a part of himself behind. He then remembered that somewhere in the past he had been told by a soothsayer that even if he were to change his name, sadness would always be his lot. This gave him pause to think a bit but he immediately dismissed such a thing as too uncertain, and yet he did not wish to go completely against it because of other things he had heard. So he considered moving about the letters of his name, for in that way he would not be changing it and would thus not be tempting the fates. He did not see that this, too, was but one more trick of the fates.

He was all caught up in these thoughts when he spied a woodcutter coming out of the forest onto the road that led to the bridge. He was riding along lying on his animal and partially covered by a horse blanket. It appears that when, before chopping the wood, he removed some of his clothes, they caught fire and began to burn. He ran to save them and in his haste the fire did harm to parts of his body. Right there in front of him the knight met another woodcutter heading into the woods. Seeing him coming out like that with no wood, the knight asked why he'd gone into the forest. The woodcutter who had been burned, speaking in the Galician tongue, answered quite simply,

"Binmarder."*

The knight noticed how in that dialectical speech the letters *B* and *V* had swapped their pronunciation and it suddenly all became quite mysteriously significant to him, because he, too, was someone who had caught fire, so he decided to call himself that from then on.

Not much time had elapsed when one of Lamentor's servants passed by on his way to the castle. When Binmarder learned from him that Lamentor had arranged to establish a large estate there where he would live for the rest of his life, it was of some relief for him; he had wondered where Aónia would be staying in that land and it had weighed heavily on his thoughts. As he put that concern aside, however, a new one came to mind that occupied him until late into the night as to what he would do and where he would go. He could not decide, for if he left for somewhere else it would be terrible for him and yet if he remained it would be impossible for him to hide from his squire.

---

*In addition to being an anagram for the author's name, Bernardim, the knight's new name (Binmarder) also corresponds, conceptually and phonetically, to the Galician phrase, "vin m'arder" or "I caught fire good," which itself invokes the image of the knight's "burning love" for his new lady fair.

Assailed by both those possibilities he remained like that, forced to more by nightfall than by what he wished, and was still undetermined when he got up. He went to get his horse where the squire had left it and he could not find it. He returned to the ash tree where he had been before and from there he went to see if the animal had gone to drink by the river. Not seeing or hearing it anywhere, he went back to lean against the ash — thinking mainly about the horse now. It was not long, however, before his true thoughts returned, and he seemed to have a fantasy where he was envisioning the Lady Aónia as he had seen her earlier, and tears of loving pity began to fall from his eyes.

Taken up that way in that sweet sadness he sensed somebody beside him, and when he looked into the moonlight that was thereabout he caught the shadow of an uncommonly huge man near him. That strange and sudden appearance made him uneasy, but, brave man that he was, he laid hand to his sword, gathered up his courage, and asked who he was. As he received no answer, he took a stance with his sword unsheathed now and asked,

"Either you tell me who you are or I shall find out for myself."

"Calm yourself, Binmarder," the shadow said, calling him by that name, "for you have been conquered by a weeping maiden."

Binmarder drew back at that, startled because until then he did not think that anyone knew him. Then, peering intently as he turned to ask him how he came to know him, he saw that the shadow had turned toward a tall thicket close by there, gone into it, and disappeared in a trice.

With his thoughts all taken up with what that might have been, Binmarder began to hear a thunderous noise coming from the woods near where he stood and soon, with a great hue and cry, he saw his horse run by with a pack of wolves in pursuit. When the horse made an attempt to leap over the stream it fell into it and the wolves were upon it, tearing at it from all sides. By the time Binmarder rushed there to help, the animal was already half dead. Some cowherds from a nearby corral arrived then, coming to find out why their dogs had been making so much noise and imagining that a cow had been killed. When they found Binmarder exhausted like that they offered him shelter for the night with their rustic words and manners. Even though he wanted to be alone at that time, given the hour he accepted. He could also see that the cowherds would not linger in looking after him because night for them was meant for naught but sleep.

So they went their way to a large cattle fold where the animals were all aroused because of the noise the dogs were making and their fear of the wolves. Binmarder followed the cowherds through the corral where the cattle were butting and horning each other. They came out at the other end, where there was a fireplace in front of a hut made of hedgeset with a roofing of cork. Lying on a green bough by the fire in front of another hut was a white-haired old herdsman who was the foreman of the drove. He was resting his head on a log, some hound puppies lying on top of him while others stretched their long snouts all over him.

When the cowherds arrived he raised his head a little and, as a man with long experience in such matters, began to ask what had happened. They told him that no cattle had been killed and they also told him about the knight they were bringing with them. He then sat up and asked the knight to sit down, making room for him on the bough. When Binmarder and all the others were seated about the fire, the old foreman asked him to tell him about the disaster that had brought him to that state. Binmarder explained briefly how his horse had been grazing when the wolves came up and killed the animal before he could rush to its aid. Then the old herdsman began speaking in a measured deep voice, trying to console him for such poor luck, saying,

"The disasters that befall us in this valley because of the wild beasts are something fearsome, and if someone wants to hear tell about them it is best for him to do so in company, where there is a measure of consolation. In the middle of one dark winter's night, when I was younger than I am now, they brought down my dark-legged cow, the mother of these other dark-legs I still have, and they killed her on me. Well, beside me I had that spotted guard dog there, and the white one, his mother, both of them wearing spiked collars. Even in such a deserted spot and on such a dark night I felt as safe with them as I would have in the middle of the day, but they were little use to me that time, shouting as I was, or to the cow, who was bellowing in such pain that it was calling together all the cattle I had at that time, a fair distance away, let me tell you. Right here, where you see me now, they came and killed all the calves I had, still not old enough to leave their mothers."

"So why do you stay here still, my good shepherd?" Binmarder asked him.

"Haven't you ever seen things like this?" the cowherd replied. "You can't get anything without losing something else. The land here is rich in pasture, which can breed good and also breed evil. I've heard tell of a big man who got all taken up with things from the other world — so unlike the people in this land, who are mostly cowherds. It's one of those miracles of nature, where two types so unlike each other could come out of the same land (only part of it is woods). This has been true for both animals and for men, because there aren't any evil ones but where there are good ones, too, and there aren't any thieves but where there's something to steal. As for me, I don't know what's worse for us herdsmen: in a land with poor pasture our cattle die of hunger, and in this other place they get killed. So things are bad for us anywhere, but it's the same for us as it is for all men. You must know, sir knight, that a person can better endure some evil done him by someone else than he can the evil he's done to himself. The harms we get from bad land we don't have to endure because it's in our power to leave. When we can't avoid it we endure it as best we can. So I say to you, sir knight, don't be so upset with what you've suffered and rest your mind by putting the blame on the land."

These words sounded good to Binmarder and had not the herdsman been telling the true tale of his life, he would not have taken them to be the words of a shepherd but rather those of someone of great experience, which makes for a good recounting. Binmarder gave no reply, therefore, except for a few words of thanks for their comfort, mentioning also that he would care to retire. When he heard this, the old herdsman ordered everyone to lie down and go to sleep. This did not take long, as the herders soon began to snore and stretch out their rustic limbs whichever way that sleep ordained.

Binmarder alone was unable to sleep, as he held in his heart the one who brought no pain to him and, even though the dim light of the stars called for sleep, it had been banished for him by his thoughts. His imagination had fixed his eyes on the Lady Aónia and as she was not bodily there, he began to weep. That was how he passed the whole long night until the fatigue of his body put to sleep that part over which it had power. Fantasies and dreams occupied the other part. And after a short sleep he awoke, all bathed in tears after dreaming that he was being borne away from there by the shadow he had seen before, and with that a great many things ran through his thoughts. And he concluded that if he did not leave that land he would then see what might become of him, burdened as he was by the woes that had taken hold of him and which followed him everywhere. He thought then that he would defy what fate had foretold for him in his dream if he remained. So great was his desire never to leave there — and since everything seemed to be telling him so — he finally decided to take an early leave of the old foreman and go off somewhere nearby where he could change clothes. Since the old man seemed to have a large herd, he would return to make some arrangements for work with him, even though some young lads that came by had already been hired, because the meager wages would make it easier for him to take on another herdsman. And that was how it was.

Here, then, we have Binmarder a cowherd, as nothing was impossible for his great love. He spent quite some time in that life, with a few bad days and worse nights. It was because Lamentor, as he went about establishing his estates, immediately ordered a few houses and no more than for shelter. And as, with the great effort that it required, everyone had to work, and because of all the activity involved as Lamentor urged it along, this prevented the women from coming out, and Aónia was long in appearing to the eyes of Binmarder. That did bring him some contentment, for what his eyes were awaiting was the thing he had missed the most. Everybody in the house knew him, however, and they all called him the cowherd with the flute, because he always had one with him as a remedy for the sadness he had chosen for himself when he became unknown. Quite often he would go along the banks of the river here, or up on those heights that render this valley so charming, playing melodies with pastoral verses for a bit of contentment to relieve his heart of the ills born of his heavy thoughts.

My father remembered his songs, and said Binmarder would imitate the language of those pastorals with great skill, or, to tell the truth, with great sadness. They were composed with sweet rustic words which, if considered carefully, would quickly reveal what was behind their making. And there was something else, in my modest judgment, where the goodness of that low style and the sense of it moved a person more quickly to compassion, because imagination lets us do so many things and in so many ways.* Of all of them I remember one, which my father said he had been singing when the child's Nurse heard it. Fate must have ordained that Aónia be made aware of Binmarder's thinking, as he was now completely desperate and, unable to go away from there, was putting together wild thoughts about himself that tormented him deliriously.

Also, as everything seemed to be as if an ill fortune had been fulfilled, things having been ordained that way, it so happened that the old Nurse was a native of this land. In times past, when she was a young girl, a very wealthy merchant (a gentleman who came from Lamentor's region), had come for reasons of love and great promises and taken her away from her land, from the house of her father, who held her in high esteem and took good care of her — even more than was proper for his station. Her beauty was well employed, however. She had been schooled in books of tales by which she was already wise (and with age she would be even wiser). And they say that when they reached the merchant's land some great misfortune caused her to lose him, but seeing her in a foreign land like that, Belisa's mother, moved by pity, took her into her own house. From there exile, but to her own land, again awaited her. How the merchant took her away and how she lost him is a long story. I shall leave it for now because I have been following a different path. All paths among men lead to stories of women. Since you are now living in this land we shall see each other again and I will tell it to you then, if perchance you still wish to hear it."

"In due time, Milady," I had to tell her, "because I could not wish otherwise. Your stories are most important to me and, furthermore, since it is a tale about women it cannot be but sad. And in that way I shall not be going against my desires, in part, because if one wishes to hear tales of sadness, one cannot truly speak of desire, because desire can only be for something that brings one relief. If the contrary occurs it will be because

---

*For Teresa Amado (115), this passage amounts to a virtual definition of the new bucolic style that Ribeiro, along with Sá de Miranda, helped introduce into Portuguese literature. More than this, however, it also suggests a theory of reading, or of readerly involvement in the text, that Ribeiro seems here to be advancing, one that implies, as per the "Cantiga do Amigo" tradition he knew so well, a surprising degree of active and imaginative engagement on the reader's part.

desire can also deceive itself many times, just as happens with all our other senses."

"We sad ones," she then replied, "will immediately call this desire an annoyance, because no one should be surprised to see how words or their meanings change in people for whom so many other never-mentioned things can change. Also, my dear child, even though you see me like this now, at an age where past griefs should no longer cause more trouble than they already have, if you judge the present by the past — and end up judging things that way still and all — so great were the things that made me sad, that bearing them for a long time has not made me feel them any less. Thinking about this many times, I say that it must be that when fate decided to afflict me, it was so that life would never be quite enough to mask grief. It measured them against each other, so it seems, so that one would not be greater than the other. In this I can understand that my grief will not grow greater than the time of life left to me. Please forgive me for getting away from the subject and talking about myself like this. I will still keep my promise to you, for every woman must bear her own sorrows. It is just a matter of how I behave: I set out to do one thing and I do something else. Many are the times I have been ashamed of myself for this."

"You cannot, Milady," I replied, "do anything in my presence that would cause you to beg my pardon. Rather, the more things I hear from you the more they make it seem that you have come here only so that I might hear them. Until now I went about frightened with myself at how so much sorrow could endure after its cause had ended. How was I to spend time with other matters that concerned me? As I could not see this in my sorrow, I turned to placing the blame on someone else. And why was I driven to give myself greater sorrow, or, should I say, the chance for it?"

And meaning to say something more here, I remembered that we did not know each other that well, and I fell silent, just as I had tried not to be silent before. Then, softly and pretending perhaps that she was through speaking, she said as she stood up,

"The blame one places on the one she loves always remains with her, the same as the sorrow it brought on. This is true, because I could not love you if I gave you the worst of it. I am still surprised, though, that someone who loves can put the blame on the one loved, except I must say once more, how could they do this because of the sorrow that will stay with them, which they take to be punishment but which they are really bringing on themselves. I, too, Milady, was a young girl like you. I blamed someone against my will back then. It has bothered me so many times that I could not excuse myself except by blaming someone else. It was a discord of love. This is the same as so many other acts of unreason that seek out in their torment things that should not be borne except by fate."

With these words she turned her eyes away from me, as if meaning to tell me that she did not understand — and as I was trying to hide something from her myself, it seemed like bad manners for me to hide my sorrows from such a woman, a lady, and a sad one who bore so much grief herself. As I had already tried before to tell her my meaning, I then said,

"Believe what you will of me, Milady, because I seem to have upset you. It is best for you to know the complete truth of my life, even if it is nothing but one long complaint."

"You do well," she replied, "it is also better this way as I can venture to ask you things, because I am quite fond of you now and it would sadden me not to want you to listen first. So let us go back to our tale. When that is done, let our sorrows do what they will with us, for their desire to be told is just as great as our pleasures."

And the tale went on. I said, you may remember, that I could only recall one song, one that my father said he had heard from the Nurse. That must certainly be how he heard it.

A calm had come over the area and, for a moment, the cowherd with the flute was sitting on a hummock by the bank of this stream and looking across at the other side when the Nurse also happened to come by. He was playing the flute softly, as if to himself, and as he sat there like that a herd of cows came running quickly into the water chest-deep to escape a swarm of flies. He stopped his playing then and sat as though in thought for a moment, not putting down his flute, however, but holding it up in front of him there as if transported. The Nurse saw that, and had the urge to ask him to play because it had sounded so nice to her before, but as she was about to do so, he started playing his flute softly again and in a way that held the Nurse's attention, for it seemed sad to her and unlike something a herdsman would be playing, so she kept listening until, after a long spell, he put down his flute and began to sing these words:

Everything there is enjoys its cure,
but for me alone none is to be had,
and that I know can from naught but evil be.

The cattle seek the water
as flies bedevil them,
only I sad in my sorrows
have no place where I can flee.
I cannot go from here,
but being here is not for me
when elsewhere is the thing I crave.

As long as day stays warm and calm
the cattle go about their only tasks,
by morning grazing on the grass so green,
by afternoon they laze in some cool field.
They sleep at night without a care
as everything they need is there
and only I have lost my soft repose.

Not even when the sun comes up upon me,
nor afterwards when it goes down
and great calm covers all
does my grief abandon me.
Sorrow and something greater still
I awoke with thee today,
as with thee I laid me down on yesterday.

With thoughts that this must be my due,
I surrendered full to suffering;
one day brings on another day,
one ill another, that I came to know.
If the end replies to the beginning,
alas for all the evil I foresee,
for in the beginning the end I saw!

If I was born to see my ill
and not to see it ever end,
then better had it been to have not been born
than to see myself in such despair.
But since my thoughts do
carry me so blind in its pursuit,
might not it yet be better that I learn!

Midst tears and wails
my thoughts were born,
they grew so large in so scant a time
that they are denser than a storm.
As they are not a wind-born thing
one who forgets this does badly,
for after me there is no other me.

This is how the end
I yearn for is prolonged,
as time keeps wearing away for me
and now I find it hopeless.
Fortune leads me on,
always despite itself,
and I do not know why I was born.

As he sang this last line he seemed unable to hold back his tears, and when he finished he fell silent, as though ashamed of his words, and the Nurse could see this as he put down his flute and lifted his coat-tail to wipe his eyes. Moved with such pity, she was unable to withhold her own tears and she remained there as she was. She most certainly would have said something had not they come from the house to fetch her. She had to get up. She arose and left, completely captivated by the whole fantasy of that herdsman, who seemed to hold some great mystery for her. Like something ordained to be, as soon as the opportunity arose after the Nurse was in the house and found Aónia alone, with complete good faith and without any evil intent at all, she began recounting everything to her, swearing and insisting that he could not be a herdsman. Since

Aónia knew the language of the land quite well by then, the Nurse told her about the song and how the cowherd, with his final words, had laid his flute down on the ground and with the tail of his coarse cloth shirt had wiped away the tears that had come to him. And how after cleaning himself he looked at the coat-tail, and clutching it in both hands — remembering who he was, or for some reason she knew not what — he put his face into it, and after giving out with a great sigh he stayed that way. And that was how he was when last she saw him, for just then they came to get her. She returned quite sad — and it had been a long time since she had been so moved by someone else's troubles. The old Nurse's eyes filled with tears and she said "someone else's troubles," and then she went off about her household chores.

Lady Aónia, still a damsel of thirteen or fourteen years then, with no knowledge of what love was, found tears of pity wetting her beautiful cheeks, and it was then that her feelings first began to tingle. Such is the power of things we hear at certain moments! If she had not been such a young girl she would have understood immediately, but she did not. From time to time she would ask the Nurse to tell her about the song and at other times about his demeanor, and in order to be certain, she finally asked what he looked like, and the Nurse told her,

"I have seen him other times since then, well-built and nice-looking is he, with a beard that has begun to grow out a little, thick it is and seems to be his finest feature. His eyes are blue with a tinge of gray and his look immediately reveals some great grief that is pressing on his heart."

Aónia then remembered to ask her again when were the other times she had seen him. She told her next that the cowherd was used to coming over there behind the buildings, and that sometimes he would start talking to the workers and other times he would go along the banks of the river herding his cattle, and this was the cowherd whom everyone called the herdsman with the flute, because they all knew him.

Aónia did not know him because she never went outside, but by then she was taken by a great urge to see him and to find some way in which she could, such was the sorrow she felt and so wished to hear his song. Deceived by treacherous pity like that, she was unable to sleep all through the night. Not yet aware of what she was feeling and, despite the fire that was burning inside her, she had no idea what it was. So that all of this could be confirmed, just before morning the Nurse went out onto a balcony that was a kind of terrace overlooking the buildings, and intended for strolling. She could see the cowherd all by himself by the riverbank, not far from where she had seen him before, and there was the ash tree against which he had leant that first time, when he had come out of the tent, and from where he had seen the shadow that I told you about. It was there that he would later come to die, and now it seems that fate had led him there for that reason alone, because a person's fortune cannot be changed. When the Nurse saw him like that she ran to Aónia—because fortune hastens disaster on and it cannot be postponed—and after informing her she went back to her household duties.

Aónia arose and put on an ample wrap, as she had been in bed, wearing only her nightgown. She went out onto the terrace and saw him coming in that direction. Then she immediately remembered that she still had on her nightcap and, either not to look as though she had just arisen or perhaps so she would not appear to be ill-clothed, she raised a sleeve of her nightgown over her head and remained that way.

At that point the grazing cattle began to gather around him where he was, on a kind of small knoll, and went on with their eating, some to one side, others the opposite. Just then a large and fearsome bull broke away from a different herd and started over that way, snorting and flinging clods of dirt up onto his haunches, looking as though he were going to eat them as he tossed his head back and forth. When the bull reached the herdsman's cattle he began to fight so fiercely with one of his bulls that it frightened Aónia, even though she was safe and sound and far from the scene. As they began to get closer to him in their struggle, she could see that he was not moving away, not taking his eyes off the place from where she was watching. When she saw that the bulls had reached him she fainted, and when she came to her senses the figures of the bulls had cut off her view of him. It seemed to her that he was beneath them and she again fell down as though dead.

When Binmarder saw this, because he had not seen what had happened from where he was before, his heart told him at once what it was, and although there were many reasons for him to doubt it, unsure as he was whether or not Aónia was privy to his desires, he still thought that it must be so, for great love wants all doubtful things to be true or it believes them to be true. So gathering up his strength, then, from the feeling in his heart and from what he suspected, he took the large crook from his hands and as the intruder was getting the best of his bull, he caught him on the leg with it, breaking the limb, and bringing him down. He then threw himself on the bull, taking him by one of his horns — for Binmarder was quite strong — and then, with the help of his own bull — who had instinctively recognized the necessity of his rescue — he brought him down, twisting his head and holding him there so he could not move.

All the people in the household had come out to watch because of the great noise the bulls had been making with their roars, and they were all amazed at the herdsman's great strength and could talk of nothing else. The Nurse, who had also been watching, went to find Aónia so she could tell her about it, but not finding her in her room remembered that she was probably out on the terrace, and there she found her lying down on the ground. When she reached her she thought she had left this world, and she gave a great wail, putting her hand to her face. But Aónia awoke with the cry, overcome by weakness — and with her thoughts on the cowherd, as her imagination brought on fears and because she thought that the Nurse's outcry was one of sorrow for the herdsman because she had been weeping when she told her about him the day before. The first words she spoke then were,

"What of the cowherd?"

The Nurse was relieved to hear this, and she sensed that Aónia must have fainted when she saw the great danger that had befallen the herdsman, as was customary with women. It was something far greater, however, quite previous to what she might be thinking at that time, even though everything is possible and there is nothing new when all is said and done. The old Nurse then recounted to her all that had happened to the herdsman, and when Aónia had regained her strength she got up and they both stood there for a time looking at the bull lying on the ground. There were many people there, field hands and house workers, and were it not for Aónia's embarrassment at being seen there, so properly brought up had she been, she would not have left. She did leave, however, quite obviously against her will — which she understood even if it went against her first thoughts — and she had begun to think now that if he had not been a cowherd she would have fallen in love with him right then and there.

Aónia then went back to her chamber to get dressed, but as she was doing so she caught sight of a housemaid outside, who must have gone out to watch the bulls fighting. When the maid came back in to where the Nurse was now, Aónia could hear her saying,

"Do you want to know something about the cowherd, Milady Nurse?"

Then the Nurse fell silent, having been taken by a great surprise. When Aónia heard that, she began to listen behind the bedroom drapery.

"What about the cowherd?" the Nurse asked.

"It was such a surprise," the woman replied, "I think you ought to know. I don't know if you remember or not, but that cowherd is the knight who arrived on that dawn when God chose to carry off Belisa to his bosom and who spoke to Lamentor. And I know that when he left the tent his eyes were full of tears for Milady Aónia, and that he had kept looking at her as if he couldn't help it and was trying to resist. I have to tell you that it looked to me that when he was leaving, he was leaving his heart behind. To figure things out, I followed him outside to see where he was going, and he went over and sat down under the big ash tree, there where the bulls were fighting. I didn't see any more of what he did — I didn't have time for it — but just now I watched what he did, and when I laid eyes on him I saw how he looked, and I figured something mysterious must be going on because he was so different from what I thought he was. I right away started to imagine things and I began to pay more attention to him. I could see that he kept looking over at this place here. When you two left the terrace he was even sadder than before. As for me, that was all I needed to confirm my suspicions, because I'm sure he's the very same one, just as I'm sure that God is God."

The woman was a bit of a gossip, although she could be as discreet as anyone, but because of the first trait, the Nurse dissembled, even though she knew that it all was true. So in order to undo her thoughts, she told her to stop all that because she knew that cowherd from having heard him play his flute so well one day, and she had asked about him and was told that he was the son of the foreman of a large herd of cattle and other stock in the valley, and with that she dismissed her. The old Nurse still believed her, however, because she knew quite well that possibilities are inherently powerful in all things and in love most of all.

Aónia had been listening to the entire conversation. Even though she heard the Nurse contradict the story, she believed it. That was all there was to it, except that along with her belief came everything else that belief is accustomed to bring on in cases like this. And as she immediately began to have desires as she thought of love, not a day or moment passed that she did not feel sure of her wish for him not to leave there because of some disaster, and she grew apprehensive because true love must of need have its dreads. You can see here how that maiden had fallen in love with Binmarder — which appears to be an established fact — because both had begun their love in the shadow of simple compassion and both would end in the same way.

Having made up her mind, Aónia was now unable to get any further rest. The herdsman was accustomed to roam about those parts as they were marvelously rich for grazing, so Aónia climbed up to a kind of cupola, made to give more light, that was in her bedchamber, to see if he was wandering about there. When she caught sight of him, because of her desire to see him and the conclusions she had drawn for herself, he did not appear to her to be what he really was but as she wanted him to be. As she watched him for a while at her leisure, she saw him with his head still leaning against the ash tree, staring at the ground in his usual thoughtful way, which enabled her to take a careful look at him. After a while, unable to prevent herself being seen by him, she pretended to be talking to someone in the house below just as Binmarder looked up and recognized her. So carried away was he that he dropped his crook. Aónia, as she caught his excitement, was pleased with this so she remained there a bit longer. Unable to overcome a maiden's natural shyness, however, so young and so carefully watched over as she was, and as this shyness proved stronger than her own desire, she jumped down from the cupola. She did not get right down, however, and she managed another peek to see if he had gone before getting all the way down. She kept on wanting to climb back up again and again, but could never decide whether she should or not.

Night came on earlier for Aónia that day, earlier than she had ever known. Only God knows how she spent that night! I don't wish to speak of the many things love can bring about here, so let them remain unsaid.

The honorable old lady of a Nurse understood Aónia's distress from what she had suspected all along. Anyone who noticed it could see immediately that something was different, and the Nurse became sad and annoyed with herself because of what she had told her, and she grew even sadder at having done that. So troubled was she, in fact, that she was unable to eat her supper that night.

After retiring to the chamber with the cupola, where they slept, the Nurse remembered the child she was taking care of and, as someone burdened by some new grief, she went back to her songs. She then began to sing to the child a kind of folk-song from those times, as was the custom in such sad moments, and she sang,

> My thoughts are with you, my child,
> I recall your mother dear
> and my eyes get all teary,
> bathing you with their drops.
> You were born to grief, my child,
> But some good may still come your way,
> for your birth brought
> fear of what was to come.

> Happiness had died,
> No joy you heard.
> Your mother was dead, departed,
> all of us left saddened.
> Born to grief and reared in grief,
> I know not where this ends.
> I see you child, so beautiful,
> your green eyes growing large.

> It was your bad fortune
> to be born in exile,
> so curse ill fortune
> more than this mistake.
> Here your mother has her tomb

and we our grief.
Yet it will not be for you, my child,
that they shall die for you, no.

The Fates they give no reasons,
nor do they consent to be asked.
For your father greater grief have I,
as he must blame himself.
I heard you first,
ahead of all the others,
without me you would not have been.
But did I do good or ill?

And yet, Milady, it cannot be
that you were born for ill,
as that graceful curl
hangs over your green eyes.
More doubtful comfort for me
it is to follow this same way.
May God give you better fortune
than what has come to you til now:

Because good luck and beauty,
the old tales say,
will fight one day,
great friends as they were before.
Fanciful it is for many,
but I, with many ages, many years,
have no doubts whatsoever
but that it brings on mischief.

And yet no evil name will be believed
for it and only good is sought,
while there is care for both,
for both there also can be change.

The cowherd with a flute, who was not a cowherd, had found a pole that would be a way for him to climb up onto the cupola, and he was there when the Nurse had begun to sing. He knew right off from the proper way she had with the words and their sound that she was a native of this land and a wise woman, deducing from this that without her help what he sought would be difficult, and so he turned himself over to fate.

The Nurse finished swaddling the baby as both women shed ample tears, for the child and for Aónia, who was combing the child's hair — which Binmarder could only sense, for he could not see her because of the cloth that had been stretched across the cupola for her protection. When the little girl was all swaddled they put out the lamp and both lay down. The Nurse had her suspicions and pretended to be sleeping in order to spy on Aónia — the latter prevented from sleeping, with all her thoughts tossing about from one side to the other. At times, after a bit of rest, she would take a deep breath and let out a long sigh, as though fatigued by what she had been thinking. The Nurse made careful note of everything for quite a while as Binmarder made ready to climb down, thinking it was Aónia doing this, but then the Nurse began to speak, asking Aónia,

"Aren't you asleep yet, Milady? What's the matter, can't you sleep? It's beginning to look to me that our coming to this place has brought on nothing but disasters, but fate arranges things long before the disasters start and they can't be known when they do begin. I was wondering myself what was to happen to Milady Belisa when, on that night after everyone had gone to sleep, we got up — just you and I — and quietly walked through the orange grove in the garden, where the thickness of the foliage made it even darker. We were filled with fear and you clung to me all a-tremble. We went out through that false gate in the darkest part, where we came upon Lamentor, who had been waiting for us a long time. He was filled with hopes so distant that, in the end, would be hopes and nothing more.

"Therefore it is fitting for everyone — for ladies all the more because they are the ones who risk the most — to look at the start for where they might come to be, as there is nothing so great at the start that cannot be resisted or pushed aside without too much effort. All great rivers have a place of birth that can be blocked by a foot or turned in a different direction, but in mid-course or when they have taken on strength, the whole world cannot cut them off or change their course. They will be called a trickle, then a rivulet, then a stream, and in a short time they grow enough so they cannot be turned. Everyone should be especially careful in what he does or plans to do, for it to be honorable and proper, because if it turns out well for him, then all will consider it good, and if it does not, all will consider it bad (which happens many times, because, for our sins, intentions are judged only by their outcomes). Then, at least, he has no reason to complain of himself. In my eyes it is a great good to forgive a person the enmities he carries inside, for there is no way in this world to defend anyone from himself. There is a defense against enemies, male and female, against cold and rain, but thoughts cannot be left alone nor can they be prevented, no. For one who does what he should, and it turns out to be what he should not have done, I cannot wish for it to upset him, for the loss of a desire, unreasonable as it might have been, will bring this on. What I can say is that if it does upset him, let it also give him the patience to bear it, for fortunate in this life is one who has a grief that can be borne, since he cannot live without it, one way or another.

"A person might think that this is not necessarily so in love and that it is not customary. I think it must be quite necessary, for one must consider in everything how and when and why or for what reason it is done, so mistakes will not be made so many times in matters of love, which is so subject to mistakes. How much more to blame is the rich traveler who unknowingly enters a place frequented by thieves than someone who is poor. In the latter case, if disaster befall him, he can blame fate, but in the former he must blame himself, a more difficult fault to forgive.

"Therefore, Milady Aónia, I beg of you, learn from me, someone who has seen blame and the damage it can do, someone who, like all people, is more a friend of myself than of others—in good as well as in evil— whenever a conflict with myself might come about, and then I am more an enemy of myself than of anyone else. And it would not be a surprise, for it would be an enemy in the family, as one might say. Even though it might be evil several times over for me to have to tell you this, I knew I had to, and Milady, I would rather be sorry than happy for it."

The Nurse stopped here, not because she was finished, but to take a rest. Then she noticed that Aónia was asleep, and while thinking at first that she was feigning, she took a close look, finally touching and pinching her, and she saw she was indeed asleep. It seems that she had fallen asleep, all tired out from the unusual thoughts she was having; she was young and had never yet seen anything like that before. The Nurse, even if she had led her to doubt what had happened, from what had gone on already, could sense that it was just what it was, for nothing brings on sleep in a young girl quicker than some great sorrow, just as it takes it away from old women. With that thought, with which she was in agreement, she, too, fell asleep.

What Binmarder had been doing through all this only God knows, but finding them silent like that, he could not tell what had brought it about. The Nurse's words had cut him through with fear that they would harm his cause, so his mind became clouded and he could find no explanation for that silence. All tangled up in his thoughts by what it might have been, he remained there until the light of dawn drew him away — much against his will as he still felt unable to go far away from there. I shall not speak of his anguish, for he was a man and he could bear it. I shall tell you about Aónia's thoughts, though, from which the Nurse's good words were only meant to guard her.

They arose in the morning and despite the Nurse testing her by asking her if she had been listening to her the night before, Aónia made a complete pretense and, because of her age and the love she felt for the Nurse — who had raised her — she immediately agreed to everything. Because Aónia maintained her calm and was bantering away as she confirmed it, the Nurse thought there was no worry to be had. It seemed to her, then, that it must have been that restlessness which young girls have sometimes and, because of their youth, they do things, even though their heart was not in it, that they would not have done at a different age. Because the Nurse felt this way, she went about her household duties, which were many since everything fell onto her shoulders. So Aónia was left with plenty of time and space to think about what she wanted to do, which was to make Binmarder certain of her. By piling one chest upon another, locking the door, and pretending to be busy at something, she climbed up to the cupola, and although Binmarder was not there, she could see that he was not far away — although not close enough to recognize her immediately because he paused for a moment to be sure. She could no longer bear that sort of delay so she reached out of the cupola with a sleeve of her gown and waved to him. As soon as he saw her he came quickly and stood there, stock still, unable to speak. Aónia was determined, however, and she dared to speak to him first, which was not what she had wanted to do, for she had not reached that point in her desires. But with that change in her plans from what she had thought, she asked,

"Do you spend all of your day around here, herdsman?"

"That cupola," he replied, "is it still there at night, Milady?"

Aónia, who had caught the meaning of his words said, quite softly,

"That it is," aiding the flow of her words by lowering her eyes, which up till then had been set on him.

Binmarder might not have understood the gist of her words had it not been for that, but he did not answer because at that moment Aónia had climbed down, thinking she had heard a knock at the door and, returning the chests to where they had been, she went to open it. Finding no one there, she was about to turn back when she caught sight of the Nurse and some other women of the household, and so she spent the rest of the day as God would have it. Later on, however, she surmised that the words the herdsman had spoken meant for her to look for him that night, too. She gave herself over to that hope for the rest of the day, just as Binmarder also went about with the hopes he had received from those last words that she had spoken (though more with her eyes than anything else). But I do not think, my father said, that he could have imagined how it would all turn out to be for him, because so little time had passed between them and yet, for that very reason, it seemed all the more certain, my father said, because since fortune plays a greater part in matters than anything else, anyone blessed with it has no need of other things.

That was how it turned out for Binmarder, for at nightfall, when he stationed himself by the cupola as he had done the night before, he heard them go to bed, but after a long time worrying, he heard soft footsteps in the house, as though someone were coming toward the cupola. As he listened closely he heard someone climbing up, and unable to believe it could be that (as occurs in the case of things that are deeply desired and hoped for) but, rather, suspecting some disaster instead, he got down quickly and stood beneath the cupola. Aónia lifted the curtain, but since it was so dark she saw nothing. She stayed like that for a while, but hearing nothing, doubt came over her and she got ready to go back down, saying,

"It must have been just talk."

Binmarder recognized her voice and said,

"It wasn't that and it will never be." He climbed back up to the cupola and she recognized him as he climbed, and when he reached the top, wanting to speak with him, she said,

"Quiet, or you'll give me away."

Just then the baby began to cry and it awoke the Nurse, who began to rock her, singing, but as the child had no wish to be still, the Nurse stood up, saying,

"I can't find a light. This child must have heard something."

Then she opened the door and went to the other women's quarters to fetch a light. Aónia saw there was nothing she could do and, wishing to get down, she put her face alongside the cupola and said,

"Leave now. There's nothing to be done now."

"I cannot leave like this," he stammered.

She felt sorry for him at that point and although she was moving to lower the curtain, she first told him,

"You may judge what I would have said from what I did for you, so forgive me, but I cannot do any more than to lower this curtain."

She lowered it and climbed down very carefully, putting everything back in place, and when the Nurse returned she found her in bed.

Binmarder remained by the cupola until morning, his thoughts full of the words Aónia had spoken when she left and the way she said them. For one reason or another he was unable to leave or even to be aware of the passage of time. But since he had not slept that night or during the day that followed and, resting from his cares — though not to feel them any less, because if the thing a person desires drives him that hard he cannot rest, but when a touch of assurance comes to him he can rest and sleep as though he had attained his desires (and we cannot say that the desire will be less than it was before because of the simple fact that it can only be greater) — so it was that Binmarder, partly from fatigue and partly from contentment, was borne off by his thoughts so much that his hands and feet became like his dreams and he fell to the ground, taking the pole with him. As he fell, he struck his head against the wall, covering himself with blood, and he was not well for several days after. But great events never reach their end except through great disasters, as this will show you, for that fall was the cause of Binmarder's seeing things that chance would never have let him see.

The story tells us, however, that the baby would not let the Nurse get any more sleep, so she heard the loud crash and Aónia, who was not asleep either, also heard it and imagined right away that it was what she feared, but she made a great pretense because she was suspicious of the Nurse now. The latter, however, who mistrusted Aónia in turn, suspected something else — just one of those things, because there were people all around there and perhaps one of them had come to spy on what they were doing at night — because she knew quite well that men did all manner of bold things at night. So as soon as morning came, she went out behind the houses and found signs that confirmed her suspicions. She immediately gave orders to block the opening up with stone and mortar, first sharing her thoughts with Aónia, who listened with such sorrow that it was harder for her to conceal it than to bear it all by herself, because the first is done by will, while the second is contrary to it.

But while this solution had set Aónia back, it gave rise to a quite different one on her side. She called in one of the women of the household, Inês by name, who was prudent and one to whom important matters could be entrusted. Swearing her to secrecy as best she could, she bared her heart and told her to send someone over to see if the cowherd with the flute was still by the riverbank and that if he did not see him, to inquire about him from another herder. She did just that, and she learned that he was lying ill in the house in the hillside forest nearby where the wife and children of the foreman of his herd lived.

Taking a man from the household with her, Inês decided to go there because she had seen Aónia's great desire, and this was the least she could do. She reached the forest directly and asked about the cowherd with the flute. People pointed out a thatched hut behind a group of others where he was lying. When Inês managed to have them left both alone, she told him all about her reasons for coming. Binmarder believed her at once because she was a woman, and he lay on his poor pillow and let flow some strange tears upon it — strange because they were brought on both by his great happiness and his great sorrow. As tears are accustomed to fall for both these reasons, this assured Inês of the great love he bore Aónia (all of which she did not neglect to tell her later on). They remained like that for a long time while Binmarder told her everything from the beginning. Their taking so long for that might have aroused suspicions of something evil if they had been somewhere else, but it raised none for the forest people, who would not have seen anything bad in it. Even so, they took less time than they wanted to because of the man Inês had brought with her. When they got back to Aónia, Inês told her everything, with all its details, omitting nothing.

It so happened that close by there was the home of a holy woman to whom many pilgrims came, and the next day was the eve of her feast day. So the Nurse and the women of the household had made arrangements to visit there. Lamentor gave his permission and it was an easy trip on foot. As they went through the forest, Inês went over to Aónia to point out where he was, for that was how they had set things up. Then Aónia feigned fatigue and the Nurse said right away that she should take a rest. As there was no way now for Aónia to get to where Binmarder was, Inês went there instead.

On the way back they lingered a while as Aónia found some pretext to go behind the houses, taking Inês with her. She had time to reach the house, where he was leaning up against the wall and weeping because he had not seen Aónia pass, and he might have, had he been able to get up. Having missed her then, he now thought he might miss her on her return, because no evil comes without bringing on another. Therefore he was there, weeping as heavily as ever has been seen.

When Aónia came in she paused a bit, and she heard him weeping and sighing softly as though holding himself back. In an attempt to find out why he was doing this and wishing now to know all about him, she paused again, but with the thoughts that came over him after his weeping, he went on with it, again even more. Then Aónia sat down on the edge of his humble bed and touched him. She tried to say something but was unable to, having lost her courage. When Binmarder turned and saw her he, too, lost his courage. They remained that way for some time, not speaking, he with his eyes on Aónia and she with hers on the ground, because when Binmarder had turned to face her, bashfulness overcame her.

When she did lift up her beautiful face, it was covered with such a blush that the color was supernatural, as my father said (because everyone knew this story in his time) and it seemed as if this coloring had come to help Aónia with Binmarder, for, beautiful as she was, it made her even more beautiful.

While they both remained like that, transported by their love, Inês came to the door and announced quite firmly that they had to go because Aónia was being called for. So Aónia was forced to stand up and leave while Binmarder had to watch and stay behind. But Aónia could easily tell how things were from the look in his eyes, so she lifted a sleeve from her blouse and tore off a piece, as though it were a cure for his tears, and she handed it to him, showing him in that simple way, just by giving it to him, what her great sorrow prevented her from putting into words. As she gave it to him, though, she looked into his eyes and said,

"It weighs heavily on my heart that fortune did not let me halt your weeping for something that I had not wished."

She spoke these words when she was already at the door and with them, and from what she felt as she said them, there came a flow of tear drops in two paths from her beautiful eyes across her lovely cheeks, leaving marks where they had run down, which moved Binmarder to great weeping of his own as he lost sight of her. His weeping was such that his eyes could not do enough of it, preventing him from saying anything. And as Inês hastened her along with words and tugs, almost dragging her or even carrying her, Aónia turned back toward him and said,

"They're taking me away."

As she was carried off like that, she disappeared from sight completely, the other houses cutting off the view of her from Binmarder's door. All that was left for him was to cross over to the other side of the room where, without going out, he could see the path they were taking. He stood there watching for as long as the terrain allowed, and after a good while — by which time they should have arrived home — he seemed to let his eyes rest in their imagination, too, weary of looking at what they might be seeing if the houses had not interposed themselves. When it seemed likely that she was home, he remembered where she had been sitting and ran back there and began to imagine every tiny detail of what she had done.

Then he picked up the piece of sleeve she had left him and he began to weep into it, along with some words, as if she were there to hear them. That was how he passed the time of his illness, visited by Inês many times until his recovery.

It was at this point that the misfortune of which I shall tell you came about, along with countless other things that occurred. Lamentor's estates were limited and isolated, and because of this isolation Aónia, the Nurse, and other women of the household would go out to spend time along the riverbank, where Binmarder was always about. But no one should place a great deal of trust in anything of this world, nor for the great security that Binmarder felt in such a secluded place, which was not to last long for him, as you shall see.

It so happened that the maiden for whom the knight of the bridge had died had come to a sad end herself, thanks to the widowed sister who had carried him off in the litter. And also there happened to be in the castle there the son of a most worthy and wealthy knight of that land. He who had let it be known to neighbors that he wanted Aónia as his wife, a decision in favor of their marriage being based on their equal status.

Because of Lamentor's unhappy state of mind and from the isolation of her life, Aónia did not learn of this until the day before they were to take her to this castle, for Lamentor, although not wishing to see any pleasure in his house, nevertheless found it agreeable that Aónia should not be displeased with her husband, a knight with a fine reputation and well provided with life's worthy goods. He had refrained therefore from mentioning anything to Aónia at the time. That was not how it was, however, because Aónia spent the whole night wailing, and had it not been for Inês, who knew full well about her secret, she would have died or gone off into the forest we see there. But Inês consoled her and gave her other hopes, convincing her not only to forswear any harm to herself but even to be glad about that life and to want it, for she told her that for all marriage occupied men, she would have all the freedom she wanted, which was impossible for her to have in the household there. This advice was accepted without consulting Binmarder because there was no time for it. So they arranged for Inês to stay behind and tell him. The next day or the one following Aónia would send for her, because she planned to request her services from Lamentor.

That day after came, and as Binmarder was not yet herding cattle he was up and walking along the riverbank even before dawn, and he saw a great many people coming along on horseback and crossing over the bridge to Lamentor's estates. There was no one around whom he could ask about it, but he remained there as his thoughts began to turn and he wanted to find out what it was all about. More often than not what first comes to mind, if we harbor a suspicion, will quickly let us understand all or some part of what it must be. After dismounting, the people on horseback spent a long time with Lamentor, and when they began emerging, one by one, their faces showed signs of pleasure. It was then that Binmarder saw ladies on horseback, and he saw a long line of people heading toward the bridge, where he had a chance to ask a page what was happening, and the boy answered him as he made his way along the path. Binmarder could not bring himself to believe it, so great a blow was it to his heart. But then he saw Aónia, and alongside her on the left was her husband, whom Binmarder could recognize both from his attire and from the way they were chatting with each other. He saw it all, finally, and he understood quite well. Aónia never turned in his direction, not because she was sure of him, as she had been always, but because she was turned toward the side on which her husband was riding. Binmarder thought she was acting in a more exaggerated way than she really was, and he thought therefore that she was doing it to spite him. And as is natural when a person makes a mistake, he thinks the worst afterwards, as happened here. Binmarder was so wounded that he could think of nothing else for more than an hour and he finally went off, never to be seen again.

That same day Inês went to look for him, and when she didn't find him she made enquiries about him. Another cowherd said that he chanced to be near him watching all those people, too, and that after they left, Binmarder stayed with his eyes fixed on the ground and remained in that same position, like a man who was all wrapped up in some kind of inner thought. Since he just stayed that way, the man tried to say something to him, but at that point Binmarder went off along the riverbank in the opposite direction, with a rigid kind of walk. He disappeared and the man never saw him again. Then the man went back to the hilly forest where his master was, to ask about Binmarder and if he had come back to look after his cattle, as they were roaming all over, and so they all went into the forest to look for him. Everybody thought he must have run off, because he had never acted like that before, and so someone else took care of his herd. Inês was left completely at her wit's end, and straight away she thought that it would not be right for her to go live with Aónia — or even see her — after her advice had turned out so poorly.

So when she returned to the house, she arranged her departure for a few days later in order that she could see if she might learn something about Binmarder in the meantime.

But she had heard no news, and Aónia was pressing her to bring her some, she decided to go to her in spite of everything, because — thinking along other lines — she thought that with a little effort Aónia could be cured and could get Binmarder out of her mind, for although at first glance marriages seem to be something else, ladies who had been prisoners of love before, after the first few days, soon forget all about the past, and afterwards, because of annoyances and upsets born of waiting so long, any memory of the past will bring on disdain. Therefore, she thought to herself, she wanted to obey Lamentor, who, at Aónia's request, was now ordering her to go there.

What can I tell you? No sooner did she get there than Aónia took her aside, but when she learned what had happened she shed many tears and cursed the day she had been born. Inês, who was wise and knew that since such maladies cannot be cured it was necessary to delay matters, spoke to her in these terms,

"Stop weeping, Milady, for if you keep it up two very great ills can only come of it. One is that you will kill yourself from weeping, and when perchance Binmarder does come he would not care to find you like that. Then it would be an even greater offense, because the first could be pardoned, but this could not be — unless you wish to say that you had no faith in him, which is the same as thinking ill of him. So you would have none but yourself to blame, Milady, if you were to shift the blame to someone you love so much.

"Enough of this, then, for there's one more ill you run the risk of if they learn of your weeping, and because it would come about at the time of a wedding, they could only think poorly of your tears. So rid yourself of this now, with the chance that there may still be time — which I am waiting for — Binmarder's tears could only have been tears of love, for loving you so much, and he could not love you that much without your actions paining him so greatly that for a long time he does not know, or even want to know, why or how you did what you did. Because a great love makes a person feel quite keenly the offenses he receives, they seem to him to be greater than they really are. And yet it always leaves a doubt in one's belief that will come out sometime, sooner or later, depending on how great or small is the grief that brings it forth. It cannot be, Milady, but that what you know can make Binmarder doubt what you have done so that he may then undeceive himself. For if that is not how it is, then there is no truth in the world or in men."

These words were of great solace to the Lady Aónia, but not completely so, for in truth if they had left her alone with time to persevere in this thought, she would not have endured very long. But she was married then and, what with one thing and another, was never left by herself, so that her thoughts became scattered. So she was gradually becoming used to a different way of life as household matters, and the mistrust or lack of hope she had regarding Binmarder, were now casting the shadow of forgetfulness over past things, wherefore she might be able to live out the days of her life in peace — if there were certainty of anything in this life. There is none, however, for chance holds everything in tow. So let us then leave things as they are for now.

The Tale of
AVALOR & ARIMA

Arima, for that was the name of the noble baby and ward of the Nurse, had very quickly grown into the most beautiful creature on earth. What she especially possessed to a very high degree was an upright character that was part of her nature, something that in so many women must be invénted in order to add to their attraction. Her gentility of speech and manner was beyond that of any mortal being. The temper of her voice had a tone quite unlike that of human speech. What else can I tell you? It simply seemed that every perfection there was had been brought together in a way that never would be seen again. She was also her father's great and only love, and he had set aside great possessions for her as fortune had set aside so many others.

In this Ocean Sea of ours, into which this river flows near here, they say there lies an island which in those times was so abundant in rich lands and knights that from there it lorded itself over most of the entire world. People spoke of its great wonders, but that is not our story for now. They say that in those same times there was a king on that island who maintained a court of the highest rank. It was the custom for all noble maidens, as they came of age, to be brought to the court of the queen, from where at the proper time they would emerge in honorable marriage. Lamentor was held in high esteem in that land and in all those subject to it, and his fame was quite well known to the king both for his bearing, which the king found to be quite different from that of all the others, and for his noble blood and recent deeds at arms, of which he had been told by the many knights errant in his court. Thus he desired Lamentor to honor the court with his daughter, Arima, as he surmised that it would give him an opportunity to see her father on occasion, something that he wanted very much. The king also thought that the daughter's marriage might change the father's original intent.

Lamentor, who was quite aware that a royal request was a command, could not deny the king his daughter. Everything was made ready for the departure, with many kinsmen and women who had been there for the wedding of Aónia. Arima was attired properly, even though in mourning, because although her mother had been dead for a long time now, in her father's house it did not seem to be so, and it was the custom there for this manner of dress to be the proper one. When Arima was now quite ready to depart, she took leave of the others and went by herself to the chambers where her father had been accustomed to stay after the death of Belisa — who was there always present for him and which he used as a place for sad contemplation. She entered and went over to him and knelt to kiss his hand, as he took her lovingly in his arms and seated her next to him. He held her lovely hands in his, and with eyes filled with tears said this to her:

"As a crumb of comfort for me to bear the sorrow that she left me with, it seems to me, Milady daughter, that your mother left me you. Now I am pressed with further grief where there is no more room for me to receive it."

And as these words now brought on tears across his honorable beard, they brought on others in Arima, but he turned, making an effort as the knight he was, and he wiped his eyes and told her, as he sought to soothe her, seeing that her tears were flowing, too, these words:

"Weep not, my child, for you do harm to your heart that way. So many tears are harmful to your beauty as well, for you will not be able to hold onto it forever and it must not leave you before you wish it to, for it will not wait for anyone. You are going to the court, where custom calls for pleasure alone, true or feigned. Leave your troubles behind here with your father, because I was born for them. You must have been born for something else or such beauty would not have been given you by chance, for it must have been ordained in heaven. From the first, I knew that this land would possess and hold me because I have lost my better part and it lies in it. This is all I ask of God.

"There are many things that come to mind for me to tell you on your departure, but what I wish with all my heart is that you may be spared sorrows and consider them as things unseen, never meant for you. And I remind you only of this: you are a stranger in that land and everything about you will be noted and much will be expected of you, so you will not only be obligated by your good intentions but also by what others might think of them. When fault is found in a maiden it is difficult to remove. The judgment of everything can come from something very small, because the little things are what people set their eyes upon rather than upon the big ones. When they do so, they see expectations, and these come about but once in a lifetime. So be careful with the little things, my child, because the big ones are born of them and, also, presumptions and suspicions are born of them and these are much worse for the finding of fault than what is certain and true. A good reputation is the best inheritance one can have in this world. Riches and estates are proper for your king to have, but your reputation is yours alone. There ought to be less work in this for you, but still the fruits are better. In all matters, trust no one, and this includes yourself, and men, and anyone.

"Remember what I am telling you now, my child, and that it was I who told you. Everything is suspect and nothing is secure for women, as saintly and virtuous as they may be, and men go astray because of them as they go about attempting in many ways to make women believe that it is not desire alone that drives them — which is a great fraud for you ladies, because when someone has a desire with evil intent it looks to be the same as one with good intent. The actions seem similar, as they make one go to extremes, be the intent good or bad. But the basis of this mistake cannot be seen until it is too late, when no one wants to look upon it but must. This is a law that cannot be revoked, for God keeps the knowledge of a man's intentions to himself so only He and the man will know who it is that acts such with mad intent. I commend you to God's favor my child, my love, and may he look after you."

After these words he hugged her tightly and, kissing her right hand, had her rise to receive his blessing. When everything was ready and the knights were waiting for her, he forced himself to turn his eyes away, as he could not bear the sight. He led her to the door of his chambers, where they took leave of each other, he remaining behind and she leaving. After they were separated, however, Lamentor called to her again lovingly, and with a sadness filled with longing, he said:

"I forgot to tell you. Keep sending me word of yourself, Milady daughter, for there is no one else from whom I receive any."

With this they began to weep again, but the waiting knights were a stronger reason for them to say farewell than the weeping was to make them linger at this final moment.

Lamentor was left with his sadness and Arima went off with hers, which the journey and all the new things along the road would have quickly helped her to forget had she not been sad by nature, with a gentle sadness about her that differed only slightly from her modesty, both of which she possessed and which appeared only to enhance her beauty. Anyone who saw her became aware of this, or perhaps sensed it, and those who had been told of it believed it.

Avalor had known Arima's father from the days when they had been going about the world in search of adventure, and they were still great friends, so when all this came about it seemed to be quite natural, as though the reasons had been there for a long, long time, and that it was something singular, and so it seemed in both their cases, especially for Avalor. When she arrived, Aónia's husband went to greet her and he introduced her to his kinsman, of whom he thought highly, saying:

"This is Avalor, Milady, of whom you have already heard your lord father speak, for they hold each other in very high esteem. Anything else concerning him I leave for him to say, because, good friend that I am, I must make you believe it, and I would be most thankful if you were to hold him in your honorable esteem."

Arima, looking so beautiful at that moment because she had no concerns about her beauty, replied with a simple "Yes," and with that she lifted her eyes toward Avalor as a way of adding her assent to the request, for she had so many times heard people speak well of him. Then, after a moment, she lowered her eyes in that docile manner which belonged to her alone, as though she had been given some special gift, for they said that even just standing, walking, and in all her movements, she bore herself with such gentility that it all seemed to be a part of a whole, and it took place in such a way that it inscribed itself deep in the heart of Avalor. It all seemed to have been meant to be, and so it was.

So for all the remainder of that evening Avalor went about trying to find himself in some spot from where he could gaze at her and, yet, he was never able to catch sight of her again, so he went to his chambers where he lay down for the night, but with those thoughts persisting in his head and thus unable to fall asleep. Since he still had not come to the decision that his desire for Arima was because of love (the desire was there but not the decision), he became so upset with himself that his many attempts to fall asleep were in vain, still unable to believe that with just one sight of Arima she should fill his memory so completely that it had taken away his sleep. But that was what he now came to believe. One single look was enough to conquer him! He had fallen asleep by morning, however, and in his dream he seemed to be talking to himself, telling himself how those thoughts had prevented him from sleeping because he was unable to fall in love with Arima because he was held prisoner by a love elsewhere.

And that was how it was. In the court at that time there was a lady who, after the death of her father, found that the lands she should have inherited had been taken away from her, and she had come there to seek the aid of a knight who would go up against the one who had done her such an injustice. Avalor was the one who was secretly serving her because of the great honor that came to him, as it was the king who had given him the task. It seemed more a matter of respect in serving her than the love of a knight to be her vassal. The lady's beauty was one that appealed more to men than to women, with its strong, well-shaped grandeur, but she had a grace of manner that endowed everything she said or did, and whoever saw her and looked closely was constrained to do her pleasure.

But Avalor in his dream was shown a maiden so delicate that she could not have been alive. She approached him with a slow gait and, taking his hand, she squeezed it and said to him:

"Sir knight, you must know that there is one intent brought on by the force of love and another that is given by a love that is forced. It could be put this way: if a besieged castle gives itself over to its conqueror since there is nothing else it can do, there is another that will give itself up because it wishes to do so. We cannot say that both did not wish to surrender, but we must say that the first had its will forced to make the decision, while the second forced its will to decide. This is the deference you are holding without revealing it, as you take great things to be small. The first one took you, the second you gave to Arima. One had taken your body and the other, whether you wish it or not, will take you, body and soul, forever. It is only to tell you this that I have come from where I came, because you are being guarded from Arima."

It seems that in his dream Avalor was about to ask her why she was so frail like that (in sorrow for her he could not remember anything else) and she replied:

"You should not want to know the cause because you will never be any happier for learning it. We spirits have been created by the will of those we stand for, and as you asked me that, know you that Arima's will aims very high. She did not wish to tell you this even in dreams, but I have always known that you have had this thought that seems to give you sorrow, even in your dreams, and that will always look like truth to you."

And then, giving a great sigh, she disappeared. At that point Avalor awoke, and as he saw the light of morning he found his bed soaked with the tears he had wept with his sorrow for that maiden in his dream who had come to him, so frail with that lack of flesh, a lack which had given her a shadow of beauty, a sense of all that was left of the infinite other things that had once been there. Awake now, he thought of her as his eyes filled with tears, and for a long time this gave him real grief, which dominated his thoughts as he marveled at what she had been telling him of love, because the more he thought about it, the more it seemed to him that this was how things stood.

All caught up in these thoughts he was unable to reach any final conclusion in anything, for the Disinherited Lady (that was what she was called) never came to mind, except for a wish to see her, and he never thought of her except as he had seen her. And so, with his mind entirely taken up with the fantasy of his dream, he could not give his full attention to the Disinherited Lady nor to the thought of leaving her for another. This was the one thing he was unable to do, and it therefore occupied his mind for a short time only. A person who loves someone because she is doing what they want her to do, quickly stops loving her because the reasons for that love are lacking, but someone who loves only because he or she is in love with the one loved will never have a lack of love, and even if it seems to be the contrary, it might weaken, but no love can ever be taken away. Yet, as I began to say, it was sufficient for Avalor to have loved the Disinherited Lady for him not to think that he might leave her, and, for this reason — since on the other hand he saw himself pursued by the memory of Arima — he grieved for himself and decided not to follow matters along like that, thinking that in that way he might get rid himself of his dilemma.

He spent all that day with that determination, and the next day, too, but when the following day arrived, still in bed and thinking what he could never stop thinking, a knight friend of his came into his chambers to tell him to get up right away because they were going to the palace. The king and queen were leaving for a city in the interior and taking all their court with them. Everything was all ready for departure. Then Avalor sprung up and went to take a look at the road where people were already passing by in a great hurry, and to call out to those who were leaving. He was forced, therefore, only to reach the outskirts of that city and then to have to return to complete his preparations for the journey.

Thing turned out somewhat differently, however, for when he got to where the Lady Arima was already mounted on her mule, her eyes and gestures greeted him before he reached her side. Avalor made a great bow and she received him in a friendly way, telling him that she now knew many things about him. Avalor replied that they could not have been about him because there was not that much. The queen was departing at this moment and they began to move along.

There were many things here that I cannot remember, but the moment finally arrived for Arima to have discovered matters concerning the Disinherited Lady, and Avalor could not deny any of them. By then Arima was very much taken with him, and as she was sorry for him, promised that she would do anything that was possible for the Disinherited Lady, and quite willingly, for anything that would make him happy would be quite easy for her to do. This offer was made to him with that grace and manner that could only be seen in her — but she was doing it for one reason and the consequences would be something quite different. Avalor was watching throughout it all and as he looked into her eyes, everything that had been there before returned to his heart and soul. No sooner did she say something than he would immediately remember the way she said it, then she would say something else and he would remember that, too.

This was how the whole journey went, and he did nothing but pay court to her all the way to the outskirts of the city. He had been lost in himself so much that he did not notice anything until he found himself at the end of his journey, with Arima wishing to take leave of him as she could think of nothing else she might do for him. Then she noticed that he was not wearing clothes suitable for so long a stay and told him:

"It looks to me, Avalor, that you have not come for such a long trip."

"I had not planned it, Milady," he replied. "I came with the intention of only going as far as the outskirts of the city. I did not follow my intention either, because up till now it had all seemed quite short."

"Short," she answered as she prepared to dismount now, "was how it seemed to me also, by traveling in your company."

She finished dismounting and Avalor had no time for a reply, nor would he have replied had he the time. That response had left him so confused that he almost forgot to take leave of her, and would not have had she not taken leave of him — as night had now fallen, it was forbidden for knights to dismount.

Avalor went back, but not to where he had been, for he lost his way as the night was so dark. I really think that, by not going in the right direction or arriving at where he had left, it was a kind of cure for what was bothering him. Losing his way allowed him to think of the places he had seen along the road and to judge from them whether or not he was going in the right direction. Deceived by them or carried away by his thoughts, he would come to a halt and therefore did not reach the place from which he had departed until well into the next day, even though he had traveled all night, which made him lose his way more than the road itself had.

When he finally did get back, the court had all been established in that city. He arrived on one day and he went to the palace on the next. As no other desires had brought him there and he had the time, he was soon by the entrance to the quarters of the princess. To constitute her table, the princess had brought with her all her ladies-in-waiting, who were of the highest blood and rank, for she was a daughter much favored by the king. After they all had passed, Avalor managed to see coming after them, all by herself, Arima. It seemed to him that she was moving slowly, although she was really going along briskly, and this false impression could only have risen from his imagination. When she caught sight of him she came to stand nearby, greeting him, as she had not seen him for a few days. When she came up to him, standing there and looking at him out of the corner of her eye, she asked him in a soft voice:

"What took you so long, Avalor? I kept looking off in the distance for you."

"After I left you, Milady," he replied, "I got lost on my way back."

"That makes me glad," she answered, "because I thought I was the only one lost after you left me."

Those words, which she spoke with good intention, made Avalor proud, and they lifted his spirits very much because they placed him in a position to bare his heart to her — and had it not been for the place where they were, he thought he might have done so. As time had its way with this notion, however, it turned out to be something impossible.

Another lady, a good friend of Avalor's, rose from the table and came over to them, and until they withdrew after a time the three of them chatted about other things, during which he found himself carried away as never before. This was because after Arima had said those words to him, he could see that she had put her whole being into what she had spoken and nowhere else, except in her thoughts. This led him to suspect that what she had told him might only have been the result of her good breeding, so thoroughly genteel as she was in everything, and had always been. If she had said it with the intent he wished to infer from it, Avalor then thought to himself that she was attempting to reveal it with indirect words, after the other lady had come over, and because he already knew quite well that the desires that had begun to be declared only suffered a slight dissimulation afterwards. And yet, not wishing or able to stop deceiving himself any more about the motive of those words being in his favor, or which he understood to be in his favor, he decided to tell her as soon as he saw her again.

And it was with this determination that he went back to the palace that evening, but he did not see her. On the next day, however, he went back again, and then he saw her passing along just the way she had done that other time, but it seemed to him now that the gentility she had was something new after the haste of the other times and, as though he had never seen her passing before, he just stood there gazing at her. I never heard anyone say that others possessed that unique characteristic. It was something that made people who saw it think that it was the first time. Her greetings were never out of Avalor's memory and had become a part of him, but in spite of all that, and what he had determined, he said nothing at all to her. Although the amount of time he spent with her was ample, it seemed so little to him, that he went away thinking that it was because of a lack of time that he had not said anything to her. That was not the reason, however, because with the many occasions he had to speak to her, for one reason or another, he still did not tell her anything, and when he could find no other reason to turn to, it always seemed to him that he had not had the time.

The truth was that it did look like that, but not in the way he thought, because things happened that gave him no time to lose. Then he recognized his mistakes and what this did was cause him more hurt. It appears that this is the way it was to be, because in the end, with his excuses and the way he spent a whole year, day in, day out, not talking to her about anything he had decided, nothing seemed left to him, as he saw it, except what could no longer be. So when he came to the end of the year, he worked even harder at finding excuses for himself instead of seeking other means. The doubts he had were brought on by both love and timidity.

But these doubts say a wonderful thing about him: that he loved her so much he never came to understand that the reason he never told her was because of the fear he had of telling her. With true love, old and ancient, is the fear of everything, especially of what might annoy the loved one, and that made him all the more fearful. This being fearful is the first step for people in love, and therefore it seems all the greater as it is the most important thing. He did not understand this, however, or he loved Arima so much, as it would seem, that everything revolved about his love, as he alone saw it. He was only afraid that what was supposed to work would not, and his great love turned all of this into other pretexts.

So you can see how far he was able to go from not understanding to understanding, because if he understood this, he could seek out a way to know whether or not he could overcome his fear of annoying her if he told her. Since she had good friends, women who were also friends of Avalor, men would then find out, for their sins, what the women were talking about amongst themselves. Many times I heard my father say that this knight's love had reached such a degree that he swore he had never seen or heard of any love so extreme, because he was dying with love for Arima, and by the very fact of not telling her, he suspected that she knew, from what she did after she knew. This may or may not have been so, as you will be able to decide later on.

Let us now return to Avalor, with all that hardship he held inside, as he came to the end of the year. While he had always found things to talk about with Arima before, so much time had elapsed since their last meeting, that there was nothing left for him except to be carried away as soon as he now saw her.

What is known is that one day, when the princess was in her salon with all of her ladies-in-waiting and several knights, enjoying their leisure, he chanced to be standing alone at one end of the room, his eyes fixed on the door through which Arima would come, if she were to. He kept his hopes high no matter how late she might be, and when she was not there they rose even higher. The boon he wished for was different from that of the other knights, and therefore his hopes seemed different from the ones the others customarily harbored. Huddling there in his corner he did see Arima enter, and either his forces were unable to bear the weight of what his eyes saw, which was very great (as they said afterwards), or he was simply losing his strength, for he collapsed. As he was taller than any of the knights who were his equal, he made such a crash that the whole room shook. Some people there suspected the truth but they were also busy with their own thoughts and so their suspicions were not bandied about. It did not take long, however, for suspicions to be born, and all the sorrow and harm they would bring to Avalor.

And as there is no ill that does not find some means by which it can reach what it is to meant to reach, it so happened that present there, with a lady who was a friend of Avalor, was a knight of high lineage but low thoughts. From this was born all the harm that was to come later, for as that lady was a great friend of Avalor's, she would amuse him with little notes she sent him, and one of them a page brought asking him to tell her what had brought on such a tumble and all its thunderous noise. Avalor replied that it had been because of his thoughts.

The knight then confirmed his suspicions to himself, but some time later said that Avalor was secretly in the service of Arima and that the friendship between the two was kept concealed. This was said in part for Arima to hear, but as she was quite sure of her intentions and as yet knew nothing of Avalor's, she paid it no heed and just considered it gossip. Nevertheless, once a suspicion gets into a person's head it is never completely lost, even if she herself does not believe it. All Arima had to do was simply remember and give better consideration to Avalor's words and actions, which were clear to anyone who took a close look at them. In truth, when she looked carefully she could see that Avalor was most pleased to be in her presence, falling silent as he lost the thread of the conversation. At other times he would lose track of himself and never find a way to take leave of her or withdraw his furtive glances. He never seemed to have any complaints about her, with his ambling gait, his absent-mindedness and hesitant speech as he talked about all kinds of things, followed by an immediate and transported silence. She could also see that Avalor took note of everything about here, that everywhere the princess went Avalor would be there, wherever Arima's status called for her presence. In that way he managed to be present on outings along paths that brought him close to her, seemingly by accident, but he planned it so that it looked to be by chance. Above all, the fame of his love for the Disinherited Lady was spread about so openly that people no longer whispered it, and sometimes Avalor would place himself in the position revealed by that love so that by maintaining the false presumption the other, true one, might be concealed. It also appeared to Arima that he must have known what they were saying about his being secretly in her service, and that was why he was doing this. But he was not aware of it.

All these matters, and many others that are not written in this book, gave Arima much time spent in diverse doubts, because that shared friendship was dear to her, too (her love was that strong). Later, when she happened to be at a balcony window and saw Avalor pass she went out, and when he saw her alone and facing where he was, he came to a halt and could do nothing but gaze at her. He thought that as she could not see him, he could thus steal the time to catch a better look at her, because at all the other times he looked at her openly he was unable to feast his eyes on her the way he wished. He had always been prevented from looking at her by so many things, which made him think, as he moved away, that he had not seen her. And this—in addition to being the way it was because that was how it was—was also why, in the case of desire, when the thing greatly desired is attained, being satisfied like that only increases the desire. It is not that way with wishing, for once the wish is satisfied it is tossed away. But Arima, who knew this quite well, as she saw him coming, pretended that she had not seen him in order to see where he would stop, and she decided to stand there like that without speaking because Avalor's affairs, as well as his great secret, were making her quite desirous for knowledge of them. After allowing herself to stay like that for a long time, as soon as she saw that he was gazing at her and not speaking, she confirmed for herself how matters stood, because she knew quite well there was no such thing as a feigned friendship there. She then turned her face toward him, as it seemed lighted by a delicate flame, and although not angry — albeit a touch offended — her eyes fixed upon him, and turning partly with her eyes and partly with her body so that she was directly opposite him, she said:

"Either you have offended me or you are about to, Avalor."

And loading these words down with the serious tone of an offended woman, she broke off, but as she left with her genteel gait she managed a look at Avalor, who remained just as you must imagine, for I cannot tell you, wounded even more than he was as his eyes grew moist at her leaving like that. Those words had so cut him to the quick that night-time found him there still, and he would have stayed longer had not a passing friend greeted him, awakening him from the thoughts that held him. Finding himself in a situation where any suspicion might be harmful to Arima, and wanting to make sure that nothing came of it, he went back to his quarters, where he remained for several days without returning to the palace.

Then a lady who was a great friend of his sent for him urgently. He went and she took him aside and told him:

"Promise me to keep this secret and I will tell you things that will be quite important for you and for someone else, whom you love and prize seeing."

"Secrecy in everything concerning you would never be too much for me to promise," he replied. "Command me in anything new."

"I have always been completely sure of your secrecy, Avalor, so how could I mistrust you now? I simply wished to remind you. Do not deny to me that you are in love with the Lady Arima, even though I do not want you to confess it to me since you have decided to conceal it. Keep it to yourself as I have no wish to hear it from you or offend your decision. Do not let it be a burden for you that I have known it, because it must not offend the trust you have put in me, nor should you think that in denying it you would make your acts seem doubtful, for I have believed it for a long time. To love but not truly can be feigned and pretended, but no one, even if he truly wished to, has ever known how to feign or conceal how deeply he loves someone. I brought you here because I do not wish to say this just for nothing.

"I want your happiness just as much as you do yourself, and I am not sorry that you wish to go on as you intend with this behavior, except that I cannot take your part, even if I can also serve you in concealment at some time. You will come to know that in these matters neither of us holds much hope because the undertaking you have chosen is difficult. In it, I maintain that I cannot be of any advantage in anything, and also that you will be dead before you can bring it to pass, because from what I have come to learn from long and intimate conversations with the Lady Arima (whether or not you are to blame in them I say nothing), I have found that there is no desire that rules her. Never have I seen anything that free. For a long time I had felt that you were like that, too, because for a long time you and your affairs have brought down great disasters upon you. You always prided yourself in your deeds of not going where others would have gone and in that way, in the end, you fell in love. It is true that she is very beautiful and that she is greatly accomplished in all things, but she is so other-worldly that no one can fall in love with her because such is born either of hopes or of a lack of them. But you, and only you, have seen fit to enter into a hopeless war and you cannot deny it, because it looks so much that you fell in love with her without hope, and because all your effort has gone into hiding it from the world and even from her, something I never would have believed had I not seen it with my own eyes. Do not be surprised at what I am telling you because the thoughts of all men, by some special secret, are able to be revealed only to women."

Here Avalor could not help saying something, telling her:

"You must forgive me, Milady, but it is not for me to allow you to finish, because I do not know what you are about to tell me and I do not wish to offend my thoughts with the presumption that you will be left only with my silence. If you esteem me in any way, let us speak no more of this."

Then, taking his hands in hers in a friendly way, she replied:

"What is incumbent upon you I cannot help telling you, even if it should weigh on you, because our friendship has one great difference from any other. It is that I should seek out what behooves you more than what pleases you. This thing you are trying to deny to me now is already known to all these ladies here. Therefore I must forgive your covering it up from me, for in doing so you either wished or did not wish to keep it secret. But all of this is still nothing as compared to what I want to tell you."

It is said that she then drew close to Avalor's ear, but what she said or did not say was not known. A few days later, however, what he did because of that, I heard say, should not be repeated among young maidens lest they repent their pleasures or, at least, not be envious of this other matter.

Suffice it to say that the Lady Arima was the only one upon whom the fates had looked at with open eyes, because not only was she perfect in herself but also for the one who desired her, and if fortune had wished to do something perfect, or have something perfect done, where neither inequality nor the wishes of the moment would have a place, it would be for the Lady Arima at least to make use of the thoughts of Avalor.

There was a rumor, and it became true later on for those who had good reason to know it, that this was what Avalor's great deed had been, for everything turned into praise for the Lady Arima. But simply because this was the reason for people speaking about her, it affected her so deeply that for days on end she wept tears, and were it not for the fact that it would have opened the way for further presumptions, she would have taken to her bed. But she painfully kept herself going as best she could, for that other choice would have been worse. It is said that with one thing and another, the Lady Arima had come to dislike certain customs in the palace there and she wished for a quite different life, toward which she was becoming more and more inclined. This long-held determination of hers was spoken of and then accepted, for her grand old father wanted her home with him, where she had everything she wished, and he did just what she wanted.

Of her departure and how Avalor also left, following her, nothing is fully known except for a ballad from those days that tells us:

Along the bank of a river
that bears its waters to the sea,
goes sad Avalor,
perhaps never to return.
The waters lead him on
as he leads on his sorrows.
He goes alone with no companions,
having left his men behind.
He travels without rest,
finding this in the trip itself.
Opposite his vessel's course
there sank the setting sun,
giving a change in color to the sky.
All that was left to stay
was sadness.
The oars were stroked
and to their sound
the oarsmen sang this song:
"How could there waters be!
Who is it passes through them?"
The other benches then replied:
Who is it passes through them
but one who keeps
what he must not lose."
Following the boat his eyes caught
everything the light of day allowed;
It did not last for long,
the way love, too, is not long in lasting.
Looking at the sun held there before him,
his eyes cast off their weeping,
and he loosened his horse's reins
to ride along the riverbank.
The night grew quiet then,

which made his sadness greater,
as the rhythm of the oarsmen
matched his sighs.
A count of all his sorrows
would be like counting grains of sand.
As it drew farther off into the distance
its sounds became more distant to his ears
as did his sadness.
Into the water then he rode
and gave out a lengthy sigh.
From a distance he was heard to say:
"Let the waters that carry off my soul
carry off my body, too."
Just then he chanced upon
a boat moored in the water
as its owner rested.
He leaped into it,
cut the hawsers and
the current and the tide
helped float him along.
No more was known of him,
nor could any news be heard.
They thought him dead,
but how were they to know?
He sailed off to his fate
and we can only wait to hear,
trusting only in the waters of the sea.

After many years, for nothing can ever be concealed for long, his story, along with hers, came to be known, and this is how it was.

It seems that Avalor's misfortune came upon him in that land to which the Lady Arima had been taken, which was this very land but at that time. It was where a high cliff jutted out into the sea. In that small boat he made landfall on the morning of the next day, before dawn, and over the great roar of the waves, as the sea broke furiously against the crags of that high promontory, Avalor imagined that he was hearing something. And as he listened more carefully, he was sure that it was the voice of a young woman that seemed to be coming from among the crags, saying:

"Oh, pity! Oh, mercy! Woe is me!"

He gathered from this that it was coming from the land and although the voice immediately moved him to pity, he still carried a greater sorrow in himself that was even stronger. Then he reminded himself of his venture and picked up his oars again in hands that were all blistered and bloody from his trip. Much as Avalor tried to conquer the waves surrounding him, they kept summoning him to land, and when he realized this, they had already taken control of his boat. And careless as he was because of his thoughts and his struggles with the oars, he was not aware of this until a huge wave covered him and the boat with foam and flung them against the rocks, smashing the boat to pieces.

"God protect me!" he cried.

He hung firmly to one of the rocks that emerged from the sea while the waters broke against that crag with a fearsome roar and hurled drops of sea up to the sky. From its force, or from the echo of it, the wave rose up like a beacon, but then it quickly gathered itself together and all that water poured back into the sea, waiting, as the high seas swelled up again as if seeking vengeance on those cliffs for disturbing its waters. Since dawn was breaking now, and Avalor had sufficient light and opportunity, he could see everything and could protect himself. This was not what he did, however, as he turned his eyes toward the distance, and as his sight became foggy, he is said to have spoken these words:

"I am weary of so much sea and there is so much more left there."

Then, filled with emotion and wishing, as it seems, to put an end to it all, as he watched the waves around him again, he released his hands from the rock and said:

"As my body has been so luckless, I only want to follow in its path with my soul once more."

And in that way he gave himself completely over to the waters of the sea — which may have taken pity on him, for they say that things that have religion also inhabit the water. From the place where Avalor had thought to die, they quickly bore him to a cove that extended back from that crag away from the high seas.

When the waters had receded he lay there on the sandy beach for a long time, sensing that he was dead, because with the ebb-tide the sea had not yet returned to touch him. When he later recounted this to a good friend, they say he told him that he never had been so happy, for it seemed to him that he was walking along there with the Lady Arima and hearing her speak the slow words she spoke. And he had watched the motion of her mouth that only he had seen in other times, and what had then seemed so deathly seemed now to him, as he looked at her eyes resting sweetly in the shade of those brows, that love was merely taking its ease.

As he was enjoying that delightful touch of imagination, however, he heard once more another voice speaking those same painful words he had heard before, and opening his eyes toward them now, he saw that the sea had withdrawn and that he was alive. For one who had spoken so many times in envy of such a rest, he could not think of what could be happening, for how could one so unfortunate as he go on living. He looked at the crag where he had been, and from which he had been borne away, and marveled at how far distant it was. Enveloped in fantasy like that, he heard the sound of someone whispering into his ear, or right inside it, who was saying:

"Do not you know, Avalor, that the sea cannot tolerate anything that is dead?"

He looked then to see who was telling him that so close to his ear, but seeing no one, was only able to hear it when it spoke once more:

"What do you wish of me? If you try to see me it will be in vain if I do not wish it."

"I wanted to ask you who you are," Avalor replied, "and also the meaning of what you told me, because the fact that things are not as you say disturbs me greatly."

"Knowing who I am," was the reply, "would bring on a great delay for you and you have a long way to go, for it is farther than you think. What I have told you is the truth, for not being alive means being dead."

This answer was enough to make Avalor redouble his wish to know who it was that was speaking, and this is what he said:

"If there is anything that will bring you contentment, I beg you in its name to wish to tell me who you are."

"That might provide me with contentment at some other time, but I cannot wish it. You must forgive me, for if I tell you who I am it would offend the great love I have wanted, and still do, for between the condition I find myself in here and the one I might have been in elsewhere, there stands nothing but blame for the one upon whom I do not wish to bring it, and I shall not do this by telling you."

Here, and with a great sigh, the voice departed, saying:

"Sad are those who can no longer deceive themselves."

Avalor was left astounded by all he had heard, especially by those final words, which made him very sad, because in them, the voice, whoever it was, seemed to be that of someone in love. And once more he heard that very painful cry, calling:

"Alas, alack, oh miserable me!"

As the sun had now fully emerged from its bed chamber in the east, Avalor could calculate from where the voice was coming. He decided then to go there, and so he arose and was off. Using his eyes and all his senses, he went along searching until he was forced to use his hands and crawl along where his eyes were taking him on that difficult path up that same crag, and thus could reach the place from where he heard the voice. As he went along, it began to call more steadily, and when he came close to a large stand of trees high on the top of that cliff, he saw a maiden at the foot of an ancient tree, her hands bound. Her hair was loose and hanging over her face, but as he drew closer he saw it was beautiful, all bathed in pitiful tears as they dripped from her large green eyes and made marks like tracks across her cheeks. Then, as she cast her beautiful eyes upon him, she spoke:

"Help me, sir, for in that way you will be helping the one you love the most."

"That, Milady," he replied, "I shall do most willingly," and saying that he drew his sword and cut the thick bonds that held her hands. It was difficult for her to rise, so weak she was, and she would have fallen had he not come quickly to her aid, taking her gently in his arms and setting her down on the greensward under those tall trees, from where the broad sea could be seen. He cut off some branches for her and arranged them about her head as a shelter, telling her:

"I wish I could be of better service to you, Milady, but you are not the only one who is unfortunate here."

With these words, which Avalor spoke now with his eyes upon the sea in the distance, he could not help but reveal in them the sadness that his memory was bringing him from other parts — by which the maiden could see that he must have been in love, and this brought hope to what she was now thinking because he looked to be a knight, even though without horse or weapons, so she spoke to him thus:

"Although my sorrows have been so great that they have left me no room even to think about their remedy, yet can I take good hope from your coming here to aid me, for if you had come only a little later you would not have been of any help to me!"

With these words she once again began to bathe herself in tears and added:

"Woe is me, and yet had I died like that I would now be free of such great cares!"

And with a great sob, here, she stopped speaking.

Avalor, even though he had himself to look after, went over to her and said:

"Please leave off your tears, Milady, if you have need of any service from me. I, who have suffered all the sorrows that I have, find myself ready to give aid to those who sorrow, and so that leaves you no reason not to ask me except for what might bring me ill."

With her spirits bolstered by these words, although still fatigued, she replied:

"Your offer is gratefully accepted, for great is the need I bear for relief from the afflictions these great disasters have visited upon me."

Giving a sigh here, she wished to say more but Avalor, seeing now how fatigued she was, scarcely able to breathe, asked her to rest a while, which she did. During this interval she looked at Avalor and saw how sad he also was, no more than he had been before, but more weary — and that he truly was. As he thought of the task he would be asked to do, he regretted having promised her his services. When she saw him looking like that, she could not help asking him why he was the way he was. He told her something different from what he was actually thinking, and he said that he was wondering in which land he might have now found himself, for he had never been there before, and her cries had brought him from a place that was farther off. She told him — and he believed her — for from up on those heights he could see quite well that he was on solid ground.

He had come there only because of his desire to see the Lady Arima and had chanced upon the maiden there. In an attempt to shorten the time in which she would be delaying him, he said this to her:

"I can see how afflicted and troubled you are, Milady, and if I can serve you without bringing on new sorrows, it might relieve you to tell me what you wish, because then we would need less time for your rescue and that would bring good fortune to us both."

She thanked him and said:

"I shall not hold back, sir, in telling you of my misfortunes so that you may do what must be done, for if the request is just, it is of great help for the efforts of the one who has undertaken the task. And I shall be brief with it because in that way it will be a relief for both of us, as you have said."

"Near a great river that they say rises in the uplands of Aragon, I was born in a castle that was visible from all around, master of all it surveyed. I was brought up with great hopes, along with my other sisters who were reared the same. As the youngest, and not the least beautiful, I was chosen to serve Diana, the goddess of chastity in those high mountains, where she is honorably guarded by her nymphs. But when something is done unwillingly, it seems to offend some god, because afterwards there are always detours from the chosen path. This is what happened to me one day as I was hunting in this wilderness and happened into a knight who had disguised himself as a huntsman and was roaming about hereabouts. But he had been following my trail and had tricked me into thinking I had come upon him suddenly. I tried to turn back and flee, which I started to do, but he could run faster and he caught me not far from where we are now. He spoke words of love to me and with strokes and caresses he calmed me down, saying:

"'I am not, as fortune would have it, who you think I am Milady.'

"With these words he let fall strange tears down over his well-groomed beard and told me who he was and what he was called, and how he had disguised himself as a huntsman for a long time hoping to catch another look at me—which led me to believe that he had seen me somewhere else—and he said that ever since that moment I had never left his memory. He spoke all those deceitful words to me, which, even though I was far from ugly, I had to believe.

"Alas! How sadly I was deceived. What can I say to you, then? I was happy at every way he showed that I was pleasing to him, and we spent four years together in that great love, years that seemed to us at the time as mere days. Now they have ended, for with the start of my misfortune another nymph, also one who had pleased him when he saw her, was about and one thing followed another, all in concealment, and I was no more certain than I was suspicious, sensing deceit (yet who can deceive a person who is in love?). And furthering my wounds I, too, turned to tricky ways. One day after the hunt and all filled with thoughts of him, I sat down at my table and these eyes of mine showed me proof of the love between them, love that he had stolen for her from me. As I could bear it no longer, like some weary, wild beast who, coming home from far away with food for her cubs and finding them stolen, will drop her prey from her mouth and, forgetting her fatigue, will run all through these woods here around, which is what I did.

"Let these woods bear me testimony in good faith. I ran until I found him sitting in the shade of these trees here and taking his ease. He told me very calmly that it was not as it seemed to be, and he said that from his heart. That was not how it was, though, for as I came along, there was the one I had seen here. She had run off and was now on the top of a hill, and I knew she was not going far. Therefore I lifted my hands up to my hair in anger — and you can see it all over the ground here as I tore at it — and he tried to flatter me with lies and embrace me. I pushed him off and told him what I had seen and knew in every detail, and I asked for God's vengeance to fall down on him and his deceits, and turned my hands against myself as if to avenge myself that way. Then he took out a hunting snare I had made for him with my own hands in other times when I would console myself during the hours I spent without seeing him. As he unfolded it, I could see the writing on it — done by me with great artistic skill — and as I looked at it, I do not know how it was that I was suddenly there with my hands bound.

"He kept denying to me that it had not been the way I said it was, swearing so with great oaths, but as I did not believe him he went back to asking me to believe it for the sake of his life and mine. Then, finally, when he saw that there was no way to make me believe, taking God as his witness, he went off toward where the sun comes up with only these words: 'As you do not wish to believe me when it does not hurt you, I shall make you believe me when you cannot stop feeling pain.' Then he turned his back and went right off, and my soul immediately told me to go after him, but melancholy had greater power over me than judgment, so he left before I could ask him to untie me, whether he had thought about it or not. It was just that he did not come back. Then I wanted to call out right away for someone to help me, but the shame of having anyone see me like this with my hands bound prevented me, except now, with night and my spirits so weak and because I felt signs that I did not have much longer to live; all of this made me shout and it seems that fortune wished for you to hear my calls.

"You can see how this short time was all I needed to tell my troubles. What is left for me to pass through can only be sad because the one who left me like this just now deserted me for someone else. The help from you that I accept is not to avenge myself on him, because my love for him was not so small that I should wish him harm. It is for me to avenge myself on her."

Avalor was so bewildered by this request that he did not know what to reply, and this made her think ill of him. Unable to bear it, my father told me, the woman said to him:

"Am I right to think you do not believe me? For so it appears, sir knight. You must have forgotten that this you cannot do, now that you have given your promise."

"I am not doubtful, Milady," he replied. "It is just that I am trying to remove my own unhappiness from my mind."

"What is it from?" she asked.

"I shall tell you. By a great mistake of fortune, my father, while still a boy, was carried away from his native land to another far away. As a man he was ennobled from his great deeds at arms and, because of the high nobility of blood from which he was descended, was deserving of no less stature in a foreign land than he would have possessed in his own. Among many other deeds at arms he had also carried out (for there were many that he recounted to me), there was one he told me of when I was still quite small.

"Going along alone one time on a road through some high and craggy mountains, he came upon a richly attired maiden sleeping beside a spring that sprang forth from some rocks under a broad and leafy tree. Gazing closely at her face he could see that a part of it left uncovered was all scratched, as if by some angry hands, leaving traces of blood. He dismounted in order to take a better look, and also to see if she were in need of some service on his part, as the place there was so wild that it immediately brought out pity in him.

"After he had dismounted she immediately awoke, and looking at him she asked, 'Why do you dismount, knight? Maidens are not meant to be stared at.' 'First of all they must be served,' he replied, 'but if you are in some kind of trouble for which you do not wish my help, Milady, then I shall leave, because the pain I felt on seeing you like that in the midst of all these crags made me dismount to see if there might be something I might do for your needs. It seems to me you owe this obligation brought on by the happenstance of my passing through here.' 'Why should I tell you,' she replied, 'of any need I might have in the misfortune in which I find myself? Even if you were to offer help, it would be of no use to me.' 'Who was it that damaged that beautiful face of yours?' he asked. 'It could not have been done in any great feat of arms.' 'This damage, sir knight,' and she was quick with her words, which seemed to him to be coming from an honest heart, 'I did to myself, everything you see and other, greater things are what someone else did to my soul and life. I did not deserve those and they will not be seen except after much time.'

"Then, raising her hands to her long hair, which seemed to have been spared, she began tearing at it mournfully. My father was quick to beseech her to please stop. He said that he would do whatever must be done if that would calm her, telling her that he would devote all his efforts into securing satisfaction for her, and that he would die in the quest. He asked her to tell him what it was, and she told him in this way:

"'Not far from these mountains stands a strong castle where an uncle and two nephews live. They guard it for the overlord of all this land, which borders on another land with which he is at war. One of these nephews had taken me from my mother's house, as my father had been lost a long time ago and therefore, as it seems, I was unprotected. After he had held me in that castle a long time for his pleasure, a woman who looked beautiful, but was deceitful, happened to pass with another knight, whom they cruelly slew and then seized her. This nephew put me aside then and rudely pushed me out the castle gate, taking the other one to him. Just before this happened, demanding more, he made me dress elegantly and beautify myself, and I thought he wanted me to be happy in a different sort of way, but cruel as he was he ordered me out of the castle and locked the gate. Then he went up onto a high lookout with her and told her, 'I do this for you alone, Milady, and I am pleased to do so.' As a reward for those words she threw her arms around him and gave him many kisses. When I saw him so foolishly possessed by someone else in something that he owed only me, I grew disgusted with life and I came to these parts to see if I might chance upon some wild beast who would satisfy his wrath upon mine and where, I feel, I have been wandering about for a thousand years since only this morning. Fatigued more by my thoughts than my body, I fell asleep sometime back wishing to God I would not wake up again.'

"My father, who felt great pity for her, helped her up and asked her to show him the castle, mounting his horse and lifting her up behind him. Because of the rugged trail they were following they did not reach it until well into the night. He saw right away that they did not wish to open the gate nor to take the field against him, because one who treats women so vilely was also capable of acting that way in everything else. So they waited quietly in an alcove by the castle gate, over which hung a drawbridge.

"When a servant opened the gate in the morning, my father, armed as he had been all through the night, before he could be heard, went in on foot, threatening the gatekeeper and making him lower the drawbridge. Then he told the maiden to bring him his horse, which she did. After mounting, he went in to a broad terrace in the center of the castle, telling the maiden to stay by the gate. 'This castle and everything in it is all yours, Milady.' At the sound of these words and the horse's nicker, those in the castle came to the windows. That other maiden was inside there, dressed in a long gown. When she arose she could not demur from saying with a disdainful wave of her sleeve, 'Nothing here will ever leave, whatever it might be, except by the will of my lord, who is mine and always will be as long as he has eyes.' My father, when he looked up and saw the woman, fell silent, but he went right over to the castle gate and locked it with the keys he had taken from the gatekeeper. He gave them to the maiden who had come with him, saying, 'Take your keys, Milady, for they belong to you and no one else.'

"And then he moved to one side of the terrace with his lance at the ready. He was not long there when, from a more inner part of the castle and a courtyard there, he saw coming a huge knight who looked quite strong, beautifully armed and mounted on a handsome horse, ready to do battle. When he reached my father he spoke to the maiden who had brought him there, and with extreme anger said these words:

LAUS DEO*

✳ ✳ ✳
✳ ✳
✳

---

* "Laus Deo," or "God be Praised," was, in Ribeiro's time and place, a commonly used expression to indicate that a book had reached its conclusion. This, in fact, is how the Ferrara edition of *Maiden and Modest*, upon which this translation is based, comes to an end. Although there are other editions of *Maiden and Modest*, some of which are quite different, scholars now believe that only the Ferrara edition comes from Ribeiro's own hand and thus ends, in an intriguingly open-ended manner, as he wished it to end, with the reader being led to speculate about what transpired.

ADAMASTOR SERIES

Chaos and Splendor & Other Essays
Eduardo Lourenço
Edited by Carlos Veloso

Producing Presences: Branching Out from Gumbrecht's Work
Edited by Victor Mendes and João Cezar de Castro Rocha

Sonnets and Other Poems
Luís de Camões
Translated by Richard Zenith

The Traveling Eye:
Retrospection, Vision, and Prophecy in the Portuguese Renaissance
Fernando Gil and Helder Macedo
Translated by K. David Jackson, Anna M. Klobucka,
Kenneth Krabbenhoft, and Richard Zenith

The Sermon of Saint Anthony to the Fish and Other Texts
António Vieira
Translated by Gregory Rabassa

The Correspondence of Fradique Mendes
José Maria de Eça de Queirós
Translated by Gregory Rabassa

The Relic: A Novel
José Maria de Eça de Queirós
Translated by Aubrey F. G. Bell

Maiden and Modest: A Renaissance Pastoral Romance
Bernardim Ribeiro
Translated by Gregory Rabassa